Soul To Give

Amanda Leigh

ISBN:
979-8-9871601-3-8

Cover designed on Coverjig

Dorian Moore Books LLC

Trigger Warnings:

Please be aware this novel discusses subjects that could be harmful to a reader. Some of these triggers include different forms of abuse, mental illness and the term "crazy" being used by characters, PTSD flash-backs, and subjects of self harm.

Please be aware these are fictional characters and they may discuss/deal with situations or issues in a way that is not healthy.

If you are in a crisis text HOME to 7417

DEDICATION

To those who thrive in a little darkness, who read horror novels to relax, and who watch scary movies in the dark.

Leave your Halloween decorations up all year, I won't judge.

And Megan, thanks for always being the friend I can count on to laugh at inappropriate moments during horror movies!
RIP Slim Jim

CHAPTER 1

"If I hear you complain one more time, I swear to all that is good I'm going to throw your damn binder of notes out the window! Now get dressed. Riley will be here any minute and you are going." Ava darted around the room, aggressively pulling a hairbrush through her hair as she tried to slip her feet into boots at the same time. With a deep sigh, she gave up, tossed the hair brush onto her bed, and zipped up her boots before turning her attention back to me. "Get your ass off the bed and get ready!"

"I *am* ready! I don't even want to go to this party. You know I have a paper due in two days that I haven't even started yet-"

"Logan will be there." Ava raised one perfect eyebrow

and grinned. She knew exactly what she was doing. Dammit.

"Fine. What do I wear?" I looked down at the jeans and shirt I wore to class earlier, and knew Ava would never allow me to leave the dorm like this. Clearly the powers-that-be decided I needed a fashion-conscious spawn of Satan as my roommate. It only took Ava a minute to look through my clothes. Without looking in my direction, she threw a black skirt and dark red shirt beside me on the bed. I glanced longingly at my laptop before standing and ripping my shirt over my head. Why fight a war I already knew I'd lose?

There was a knock at the door right as I pulled on the shoes-black booties that I never wore because the heels killed my feet-and Riley appeared in our room a moment later. Where Ava was fair with blond hair and freckled skin, Riley's hair was almost black and cut into a stylish pixie. She had that natural kissed-by-the-sun skin tone, and the bright red lipstick she wore looked perfect. I would have looked like a vampire if I wore the same color.

"Wow, great job, you actually got her out of sweatpants!"

"Logan got her out of sweatpants." Ava grinned wickedly at me.

"Bet she'd like it if Logan got her out of her sweatpants." Riley snickered.

"I'd like to point out I was wearing jeans." No need to bring up the fact I would have instantly changed into sweats as soon as they left.

"I forgot he was going to be there tonight. Sometimes he goes back to his parents when they throw parties to get some peace." Riley continued to talk, ignoring my comment. "Watch out for Brittany. She's been trying to get her claws in him. I wouldn't put it past her to put something in your drink."

"Wow, you guys know how to talk a girl into a party." I rolled my eyes, but they didn't give me a chance to complain anymore. Each of my friends tucked their arms under mine and we left. This was the stuff I was *supposed* to be doing. Go to a party, let off a little steam, relax for once in my life. But the little voice in my head, which sounded a lot like my mother, told me to turn and go back to my dorm.

By the end of the four blocks we had to walk, my feet hurt, and I had completely tuned out the chatter that passed between Ava and Riley. When the small house came into view, Riley broke free from me and raced toward one of the many guys that lived there. She squealed with laughter when he lifted her from the ground and spun her in the air, before setting her down and taking her lips as if he hadn't seen her for months.

"Ugh, they are disgusting." Ava sighed. "Why are we friends with her again?"

"Pretty sure she's mostly your friend, and if you had someone to make out with, you wouldn't be complaining."

"Shut up," Ava broke from my arm and ran ahead to get a drink. For being so determined to bring me here, they sure abandoned me quickly once we got here.

"Wow, look who finally came to one of our parties!" A warm smile greeted me from a few feet away, and blue eyes twinkled with mischief. Logan.

"Yeah, mother bear grounded me and made me come out."

"Glad she did. It's odd to get to see your face after staring at the back of your head so much in class. Can I get you a drink?"

"I'll pass, still underage for another month after all." He shrugged with a grin and came closer, not stopping until he was close enough to whisper in my ear. My blood pressure rose as his warmth surrounded me. "Not a cop yet, so I'd let you get away with it. But we have sodas too if you don't want alcohol."

"I wouldn't press your luck, Logan." The all-too familiar voice said his name like a reverent prayer, and I cringed before I could stop myself. Unfortunately, he must have noticed, because his eyes met mine before turning to Brittany, my worst nightmare. "You think Autumn is dull now? You should have seen her in high school." Ice-blue eyes raked over me as the blond that made my high school career hell came to a stop right next to Logan, letting her arm brush his. It didn't slip past my notice that she and Logan both shared blue eyes, but hers were sharp and cold while Logan's were like an ocean, warm and mischievous. She sneered as she looked me up and down. "Oh, it seems you got more than your fair share of the freshman ten, huh?"

Hearing her mock my weight shouldn't have hurt my feelings. She'd made fun of me when I was nearly a starved skeleton. So why should that change now that I've struggled into a healthy weight? I forced a deep breath, unsure what to say, but determined to stand my ground all the same. "Brittany-"

"Excuse me, that was incredibly rude. Autumn and I were having a conversation, and I don't recall inviting you into it."

Brittany and I both looked at Logan in shock. I was pretty sure no man had ever talked to Brittany like that before, and from the look on her face, it seemed I was right. "You misunderstand. Autumn and I are good friends. We've known each other since the ninth grade. You should have seen her then, thin as a rail. I didn't mean any harm, though." Her bottom lip jutted out the smallest bit, and I did my best to not throw up at her B-Movie acting.

"That's certainly not how I would expect a friend to speak to another friend. Now if you'll excuse us," he turned his back to her and touched my elbow, "I promised this one a tour. See you later, Brittany." He didn't look back, and I resisted the urge to turn my head as he led me into the house and toward the back, where it was quiet. "Sorry to manhandle you there, I just can't stand people like that. If Brittany was a guy, I could at least punch him to shut him up." He let me go and sat down on a chair, motioning for me to sit beside him. I wanted to tell him I could deal with whatever Brittany wanted to say if it meant he would touch me again, but I bit my tongue against the words. "So you had to deal with her throughout high school?"

"Yeah, and I wish I could say she's not that bad when you get to know her, but I don't like to lie. Her parents split, and I don't think it was an easy divorce. She kind of became a monster after that. I felt bad for her for a while, but then I took the brunt of her attention and I kind of lost my sympathetic bone."

"Can't blame you there. So how are you doing on your paper for Psych?"

"Must admit, I haven't started yet. I had some stuff due for my other classes and I put this one aside. Had hoped to get to it today, but of course Ava was not about to let me get out of coming."

"Ouch, maybe I should brew you some coffee or something to get you through tonight-"

"Logan! What are you doing hiding back here? Come on, man, Jason is about to set up his guitar."

"They have summoned me." My imagination made his sigh sound disappointed. He stood as his friend rushed back from the room, but he hesitated at the door. "You come get me if Brittany causes any more trouble, okay? I'll be happy to rescue you again."

"I've been dealing with her since ninth grade. I think I can rescue myself." My voice sounded sharp to my own ears, but he didn't seem to notice.

"Oh, I don't doubt that." He smiled in a way that

made my heart stutter, like there was something else he wasn't saying, but then he gave me a small nod and left me alone. Man, I sure know how to party.

As if sensing my sudden loneliness, my phone buzzed in my pocket and I saw my dad's face staring back at me. Any other college student would answer their dad calling them at a party, right? "Hey Dad, what's up?"

"Hey sweetheart, I just wanted to see if you would be free to meet me for lunch next week? I know you have a free day Wednesday, but if you're swamped-where are you right now?"

"Ah, sorry, Ava dragged me to some party near our dorms. Can you hear me, okay?"

"Yeah, just a lot of background noise. Be careful, okay? You aren't drinking, are you?"

"Dad. I'm fine. Currently, I'm sitting in a room by myself. I'm a real party animal."

He sighed on the other end and I could practically see him rubbing his forehead. "I know, I'm sorry. I just worry. Anyway, are you free next week?"

"Yeah, I'll have some studying and stuff to do, but I can spare some time to have lunch with my dad. Just text me Tuesday when you think you'll be heading here, and I'll make sure I plan my day accordingly."

"Sounds great. I'll let you get back to it. Be careful. Love you."

"What are you doing on the phone? You are aware you are at a party, right? I've been looking everywhere for you and you're sitting alone talking on the phone! What am I going to do with you?" Ava appeared in the doorway with her hands on her hips. Full mother bear mode.

"Well, I just had a great make-out session with Logan. He dragged me back here to be alone, but we got interrupted. He said he'd be right back for me." I take not-so-secret pleasure in her shocked expression. "Just kidding. Though Logan brought me back here and got pulled away, we were just talking."

"Ugh! Only you would talk to a guy at a party rather than make-out with him. Come on, my cup is already empty." She grabbed my hand and dragged me into the kitchen so she could get a refill of beer.

The party was quickly picking up, and the house was getting crowded to the point of it getting hard to move. I glimpsed Brittany, and she glared back in my direction before grinding against the guy she was dancing with. The entire house vibrated with the sound of the band playing. I could feel it thumping in my chest and couldn't help but move to the music. I searched the nearby bodies and hoped to catch a glimpse of Logan. At the moment, with the dark room, flashing lights, and thumping base, I felt like I could do something dangerous tonight.

Unfortunately, he was the only one I wanted to do anything with, and I couldn't find him in the sea of people. For all I knew, he could be up in a bedroom with some other girl. I didn't really know him, not more than a passing friend. He could have a sea of girls at his beck and call. He was certainly good looking enough for it.

Ava was lost to me again, having danced past me with a drink in hand. She immediately got swallowed up by the crowd. I thought longingly of my paper and sweatpants. The music was good, but I could blast music in my room. My gaze finally snagged on Logan from across the room, and he seemed to sense me because he looked up and my breath caught when he threw a smile my way. Someone should really tell him how dangerous those smiles were. He shouldn't go around sharing them like they meant nothing. I almost went to him, or motioned for him to come to me, but fear had me pulling my gaze away and moving into the crowd before I did something stupid.

I passed by Ava, but she was deep in a dance with some chick. Even if I was too chickenshit to have fun, it didn't mean I needed to stop others from their joy. I didn't like that she had another drink in hand, but I was called a stick in the mud enough to just keep my mouth shut. Riley caught sight of me and waved, her cheeks flushed and lips perfectly swollen. Levi stood behind her, his gaze dark and watching her with hunger.

"I've been looking for you guys! We wanted to head out. Did you still want a ride back?" Riley looked back at Levi and a grin broke out on her face.

"Yeah, Ava was just over here." Thank goodness. My feet wanted to break free and murder me. A pointy heel to the eye would be one way to go. I found her after a quick search, sandwiched between the same girl from earlier with a guy at her back, and pulled her away so I could scream in her ear over the beat of the music. "Riley and Levi are leaving. We should go so we don't have to walk home."

"I'm still having fun! You can go. I'll find my way back." She put a wet kiss on my cheek, and I eyed the guy she'd been dancing with. No way in hell was I leaving her alone.

"Ava, we've been here a while. Why don't we just go?"

She was already trying to pull free, but I held her tight.

"I'm not going yet, Autumn. It took me longer to convince you to come than we've actually been here. There are free drinks, good music, and a room full of hotness. I've had a hell of a week and I just want to have a little fun, okay?" She pulled free, and I lost her. Dammit.

Riley hadn't followed me, but she watched, so I just shrugged in her direction and waved her on. If I had to walk across this floor one more time in these shoes, I was going to rip them off and throw them across the room. I'd probably kill some innocent bystander with a heel to the temple, and who knew what was on these floors. Riley waved goodbye, and I caught sight of Levi's hand going to her ass as they made their way to the door. Knowing I was going to have a battle in front of me with Ava, I found a place to sit and hid myself in a "quiet" corner.

If this was the college experience, it could suck it. When my feet finally felt a little better, I stood to get a soda from the kitchen. The brighter room startled me for a moment, but it was easy enough to find the sodas and I welcomed the sugar rush. I had a long night ahead of me if I was still going to try to bang out a paper tonight. My mind was far away and plotting when someone's hand found my ass and I slapped them away. I turned and found a guy hovering over me, moving to corner me against the counter.

"Back the fuck up." I pushed him away and, even though he was quite solid, he bounced away like he was nothing more than a fly. "Maybe you should back down on the drinks for the night, bud."

"Ah, the prude strikes again." A light, feminine giggle clawed at my back. "No wonder Logan hasn't tried to do anything with you." Why did I deserve this crap?

"Brittany, last I saw you, there was a tongue shoved down your throat. I'd say things haven't changed for you since high school. At least this time it's a fellow student and not the janitor." It was a low blow, but I was losing patience quickly. Her cheeks flamed. To be fair, the janitor they had caught her with was a college student and it'd been our senior year, so the age difference hadn't been that bad, but the school had enjoyed the scandal.

"Be careful with that soda. I hear it burns like a mother when it comes back up." She tossed her hair like a preppy bitch straight out of a movie and disappeared into the darkness. Over the evening, I went on a search for Ava again. After a long search through grinding bodies, I finally found her dancing with someone I didn't recognize, and I realized she was pretty far gone. "Ava, we need to head back. We have a long walk."

"Come on, Autumn." She rolled her eyes at me and the guy she was dancing with gripped her hips tightly, pulling her back to be flush with his body.

"We need to go. I'm done babysitting. I have stuff to do tonight, and it's getting really late." To say this night was pissing me off would be an understatement. I wouldn't be a good friend if I just left her at the party, but every second we stayed, she got more drunk, and I was not about to carry her back to our dorm. "Ava, we are leaving now. I'm not playing around."

"Oh no, is someone having a good time? Don't they know Miss Autumn Crowe doesn't like it when people have a good time?" Brittany appeared beside me again and I almost lashed out. "Why don't you just leave your friend here? I'll keep an eye on her."

"Yeah, I'm sure that's what you would do. Out of the kindness of your heart, right? Why don't you stick your nose in someone else's life for a change, okay?"

"Sure, I'll go find Logan. It's getting late and I wouldn't want him to go to bed alone."

"Yeah, you do that." As soon as the wench from hell

started away from me, I turned back to Ava. Fed up, I grabbed her wrist and pulled her from the grasp of her new friend.

"What the fuck, man?" The guy slurred as he lost his dance partner.

"You like her so much? Fine, what's your number? I'll have her call you tomorrow; but you aren't getting fucked tonight." He held up his hands and disappeared into the crowd. Typical. "Come on, Ava." I grasped her hand, and she finally followed without argument. As soon as we made it outside, I wished we had a car with us. The crowd was getting rowdy as it grew later, and we were going to have to make it four blocks in heels. Ava dragged behind me as she tried to maneuver the difficult task of one foot in front of the other and I regretted my decision to make friends.

"Hey! Wait up!" I turned and watched as Logan ran to catch up to us. "I saw you guys leaving. You didn't drive here?"

"No, Levi was supposed to drive us home, but he and Riley took off an hour ago. Ava refused to leave with them, so I stayed behind with her." Logan searched Ava's drunken face, and he frowned. "I'm not about to let you guys walk all the way back to your dorms. Let me drive you."

"Thanks, but I think it would be a little hard for you to get a job in law enforcement with a DUI on your record. We'll be okay."

"Thanks for your concern," his lips twitched, "but I've been drinking soda all night. It's not exactly doctor recommended, but I'm safe to drive."

"Really? This is your party and you aren't drinking?"

"I live by the firm belief you don't have to get drunk to have a good time. I agreed to this party so I could hang out with some friends and have a little fun after a few weeks of tests and papers. Stay here. I'll pull my car around." Before I could argue, he started jogging away from me. Ava groaned and leaned her weight against me, and I had to admit Logan and his car were a godsend.

CHAPTER 2

"I don't feel so hot..."

"Don't you dare throw up in Logan's car. He'll never speak to us again." I met his eyes in the rearview mirror and clutched Ava closer as he slowed to a crawl to go over a speed bump. For four blocks, it seemed to take an hour to get there. Logan was driving as slow as he could as Ava continued to decline. It seemed as soon as she stopped moving and drinking, the alcohol had hit her like a punch in the face. Painful memories clawed at me as I looked into her glassy eyes, but I tried to push them aside. I knew what was coming next, and we had a long night ahead of us.

"Are you okay?" Logan finally parked and opened the door for us. Without asking, he tucked his arm under Ava's opposite side, and together we helped her toward the dorms.

"I'm fine. I have a feeling I'm going to be up all night holding back her hair instead of getting to my paper, though."

"You guys really need to get to the making out part." She slurred between us. Maybe a random bolt of lightning would just shoot out of the sky and kill me on the spot. Thank heaven for small favors, though, because Logan didn't seem to hear her. He took full support of Ava while I unlocked our door, and then he helped her to her bed. Ava slumped over, her blond hair spreading across the pillow. "The world is spinning."

"It's okay honey, just close your eyes. I'll get you some water to drink."

"I'm sorry, Autumn. She shouldn't have had so much to drink. You deserve a night to relax and you didn't exactly get that, did you?"

"It's not your fault. I lost sight of her for a while there, but every time I saw her, she had a cup in hand. I should have cut her off myself." I'd thought about it too, but after everyone had told me what a buzzkill I was, I'd bitten my tongue and took a step back instead. Now I was going to pay the price, right along with Ava. "Thanks for the ride home. It would have taken me forever to get us back here."

"You shouldn't have even thought about walking alone this time of night, especially after everyone has been drinking." He took a step forward and gripped my arm, his eyes concerned as he looked me over. My heart went into a wild dance and I knew my cheeks were blazing under his gaze. "I want you to be safe. You can always call me if you need something, okay?" He waited until I nodded before he continued. "Are you going to be okay with her tonight? I can hang out a little longer."

"I think it's probably better if you head on back. We shouldn't both have to suffer the reign of puking, which will probably follow the evening's events. Thanks though." He still held my arm, and for just a moment, I thought he might lean in and kiss me goodnight. Instead, his eyes turned back toward Ava, groaning on the bed, and he nodded.

"Don't forget to call me if you need something though, okay?"

"Sure." With one more squeeze to my arm, he released me with a goodnight and then I was alone with my very drunk roommate.

"Autumn-" Ava gripped her stomach, and I moved quickly, grabbing a trashcan and moving it under her head just in time for the retching to start. If only that lightning bolt had hit me on the way up.

The next morning, I felt just as hungover as Ava looked. Neither one of us got a wink of sleep, and we both had lectures we needed to get to. It took all my willpower to get out of bed, which I'd probably only spent an hour in the night before, and dragged myself down the hall for a shower.

"Ava, honey, are you going to get up?" I gave her shoulder a nudge, but she only gave a small groan in response. I grabbed a water bottle from the fridge, and some Advil, and gave her shoulder another shake. "Take this for me real quick, okay?"

"Stop screaming at me." She forced her eyes open and finally sat up. I made sure she downed half the water before I finally nodded. "There are some granola bars in the basket on top of the fridge. Drink lots of water, okay?" She nodded, so I finally grabbed my bag and started my walk to class. When I got down the two flights of steps, I found Logan standing outside the door of the dorm house.

"Good morning! Glad to see you are going to class. I wasn't sure you'd make it. No, Ava?"

"Wh- what are you doing here?" I one-hundred

percent blamed Ava for the baggy shirt I'd thrown on, and the rat nest I had for hair at the moment.

"Just wanted to check on you this morning, and we have class together, so I thought I could walk with you. Is that okay?" He suddenly looked unsure, and I realized I was still gaping at him.

"Sure, sorry, I didn't really get a lot of sleep. I guess I should have gotten up a little earlier to get coffee...what a conundrum that is."

"I really am sorry about last night."

"It's not your fault Ava can't control herself. Anyway, how was the rest of your night?"

"Okay, I guess. It took forever to get everyone to leave. It was probably around four before everyone cleared out. There is a lot of cleaning to get done, but I guess that's part of living off campus, right? You become one of the party houses."

"I guess. I've never been much for parties and I have to say you guys didn't exactly convince me otherwise."

"I guess it's just part of the college experience. You've had the night of holding back your friend's hair and losing sleep, so you can now check that off of your college to-do list."

"Goodie, I love getting things checked off my list." I grinned, liking how at ease I felt with him. Ever since the first day of class, I had trouble keeping my eyes off of him. Somehow, over the course of the semester, we chatted and became friends. Even though I wouldn't mind more with him, it was nice to enjoy his company all the same.

We got to class, and he took his usual seat two chairs behind me. There were still a few minutes before class started, so I took out my phone to text Ava about eating and drinking water but found Riley sent me a message.

Riley: What the hell happened last night? Is Ava ok?

Me: She's fine, drank too much, and is sleeping it off. Why?

Riley: FB, Insta, Brittany. Need I say more?

The professor walked in and started talking, but now my heart was racing. Ignoring her, I pulled out my laptop and signed on to my social media page. I wasn't friends with Brittany on Facebook, but we had mutual friends, and she hadn't made her posts private. Picture after picture of Ava drinking, dancing, and making out with some guy took up the feed. I felt sick, and it got even worse when I caught some of the comments about the "slut" in the picture. The fact she was also underage, she was only twenty, the same as me, made me think there might be even more trouble than her name being dragged through the mud.

I was going to have to find Brittany and talk her into taking everything down. I couldn't stop people from sharing the pics, tagging her in them...my mind ran away with everything that could happen. Not to mention Logan and his friends could get into trouble for serving a minor. What was Brittany thinking?

The professor was just getting into the lecture, putting the notes on the screen, but there was no way I could sit idle while Brittany tried to pull apart everything I cared about. Maybe Riley hadn't been too far off when she said she wouldn't put it past Brittany to put something in my drink.

"Miss Crowe, class has just started. Am I interrupting a prior engagement?" Professor Knope raised a brow in my direction as she questioned me. I glanced quickly at Logan and found him frowning.

"No, I wasn't feeling well, but I wanted to come to class, but I feel really sick. I'm so sorry." Before she could even respond, I darted from the room. Nearly running down the hall, trying to stuff my laptop back into my bag as I pulled out my phone to call Riley. "We have to do something!" I said the second she picked up the phone. "How do we get her to take it down?"

"I don't think there is anything we *can* do...I guess just try to talk to her and ask her. Did you see all of them?"

"I don't know." I pinched the bridge of my nose, narrowly avoiding running into someone. "I saw enough. She wanted to party and dance, but I should have taken better care of her-"

"It's not your fault. I left you guys there, oh god. There is one of Logan helping you two into the back of his car. I really don't think you want to know all the comments attached to that one. This isn't good, Autumn."

"I don't know her schedule at all. It's not like we are friends. But she's in the dorm house across campus, right? By the library? Maybe I can just go there and wait for her to come back. Hopefully, it won't take too long."

"Okay, Levi is leaving for class now. I can meet you?"

"No, it's okay. Just go to my dorm and check on Ava. There is no point in both of us sitting on the steps for who knows how long. Maybe see if there is anything you can do to get the pictures down..."

"On it. Talk soon."

I changed direction so I could start heading toward the library and almost walked right into Logan. "Whoa." He caught my arms and if I wasn't so distracted by all the drama, I would have savored the touch.

"Sorry, what are you doing out of class?"

"Seeing why you ran out looking like a ghost. Is Ava okay?" He scrunched his brows together in concern, his hands still holding me.

"Not exactly. Brittany posted pictures of her all over Facebook. She's clearly drunk in them, and there are some of her making out with someone, and apparently one of you helping us in your car. It doesn't look good. Riley is going to see if she can get them down, but I'm going to Brittany's dorm to talk her into taking everything down. We could *all* get into trouble if the wrong people see them." I thought of my dig about the janitor, and my chest constricted with guilt. He let out a small puff of air as everything I said sunk in. "Logan, let me go. I have to get over there. I don't know her schedule, and the longer the pictures are-"

"Wait." He let go and pulled out his phone. With a roll of his eyes, he showed me a selfie of Brittany blowing a kiss on the phone. Instead of a name, the contact read: call me. "She put it in last night. Think I pissed her off when I didn't immediately follow up by dragging her to my room." He put it on speaker and fidgeted as it rang.

"Hey there. I was worried you wouldn't remember that I put my number on your phone." Her voice was coy and sickly sweet. I wanted to snatch the phone from his palm and toss it in front of a train.

"Brittany, you have to take down those pictures of Ava. She's underage. You could get me into serious trouble! What the hell were you thinking?"

"Hey, I took some pictures of a party I was at. I don't see the problem."

"What do you think you're doing? You want me arrested? Kicked out of school? What, because I didn't want to fuck you?" His voice rippled with anger. He had been so calm it took me by surprise, but I shot him a look. If he pissed her off, she would only make it worse. She would probably forward the pictures straight to the police or the criminal justice department head at the school. Why had I agreed to go to that stupid party?

"I have no idea what you are talking about, Logan. I was just making friends at a party. They are my pictures. If you really have a problem with them, why don't you come over, and you can show me exactly which ones to take down?" I opened my mouth to respond, but he held up a hand, cutting me off just in time.

"I'm coming right over, Brittany. This isn't a joke." He disconnected and stared at the phone for a solid minute before he finally looked up at me. "You should go and check on Ava. Try to keep her off the computer. I'll get Brittany to take it all down."

"You're just going to go over there?"

"What do you expect me to do?" He raised his voice, and a few people glanced over. I was used to voices being raised and my body reacted automatically, hackles rising as I stood my ground. My change in demeanor seemed to make him realize his own anger, and he let out a ragged breath. "I'm sorry. This is more than Ava having her name dragged around. We could really get in trouble. Usually it wouldn't be a big deal that someone took pictures at a party, but she is clearly trying to get a rise and use Ava as bait."

"I think I should go with you. She might drug you and take advantage or something." I was dead serious, but he laughed and shook his head. Then his normal smile was resting on his face once more, where it belonged, and just as dangerous as always.

"I can hold my own, I promise. I'll call you as soon as I escape. You should probably use your free period to work on that paper of yours." Then he leaned down and kissed my cheek. I stood frozen to the ground as he started jogging toward Brittany's dorm.

Had that actually just happened, or was the stress making me hallucinate? I touched the spot on my cheek, and finally forced my mouth closed. I was halfway to my dorm before I wondered how he knew where Brittany lived.

CHAPTER 3

The next few days went by in a blur. Logan convinced Brittany to take the pictures down, but it didn't stop some people from talking and making rude comments about me or Ava. I was just grateful it passed quickly, as new things came about to distract people from something that happened at a party. Other than thanking Logan after he called to let me know Brittany took everything down, we hadn't talked. He came into the next psychology class right as Professor Knope arrived, so he rushed to his seat. Other than a moment of eye contact, we didn't get the chance to talk.

"I'll see you after your classes!" I yelled after Ava as she donned sunglasses and blew me a kiss. I checked my hair in the mirror once more. I never learned the tricks of doing my hair or makeup, which left me to fumble around with irritation every time I wanted to actually look nice. Today, I had my thin blond hair pulled to the side in a little knot, but other than a quick application of mascara, I hadn't bothered with makeup. It was just lunch with my father, and I wasn't expecting to run into anyone I really wanted to impress.

"Tell your dad I said hi," Ava said before closing the door behind her. We didn't really talk about what happened. She'd seemed to bounce back from it as soon as she found out about it. She had been too hungover to deal with the stress and fear of what Brittany could do to us, and she wasn't head over heels for the guy that might have had to sell his very soul in order to stop it from getting worse. Her ease over the whole ordeal only pissed me off more, so I tried to keep my thoughts at bay. I didn't have a lot of friends, after all; I couldn't really afford to go around telling off the few that I had.

I stepped outside to a blast of cool fresh air, which I desperately seemed to need. Dad would pick me up, but I still had a few minutes, so I leaned back on an open bench and just took in the bustle of activity. People were heading in every direction: on foot, on bikes, in cars. I kept a special watch on those walking with faces hidden behind a phone, waiting to see if they walked into a sign or something. I was so drawn into watching them, I almost didn't hear my dad call out to me from his parked car.

"How are you doing, sweetheart?" He smiled when I gave his scratchy cheek a peck before I buckled up.

"Good, looking forward to next year when I'm allowed to have a car on campus. This whole, depending on everyone else to drive me around, is for the birds."

"At least there is a lot of stuff close to you. But you know you could always move back home. You'd have your car back, the quiet of your room-"

"Dad."

"I'm just reminding you that you have options." He drove in silence for a while. We agreed to go to a restaurant a little farther away from campus, if for no other reason than to let me see there was still a world outside of the college town I now lived in. His radio quietly sang out an oldies band. I recognized the song, but couldn't remember who they were.

"Are you lonely?" I finally asked. Sometimes I wasn't sure if he kept pressing me about coming home for my health or for his.

"Sweetheart." He sighed heavily, and I noticed his

hands gripped the steering wheel a little tighter. I was used to having older parents, but after not seeing him for over a month, he suddenly seemed even older. He had large hands with thick calluses from his previous construction work, and the hairs on his fingers were almost invisible now that they were turning gray. His once black hair was now a mixture of salt and pepper, though it was still thick with no sign of balding. "That's not for you to worry about. Of course I miss you, and the house is a little quiet, but we all have our adjustments. You know I have my friends, and I'm perfectly capable of entertaining myself. I'm just giving you a hard time, that's all."

"Okay, you know I love you, right?"

"Of course, just not as much as I love you." He reached over to pat my head, which made me both cringe and giggle. At sixty-three, the guy deserved to slow down, but he had other ideas. Ten years ago, he started his own construction business - which was no small feat - all while raising a teenager as a single parent. Many of my peers spent their time complaining about their parents, undeserved groundings, overprotectiveness, nagging, but I never joined in. I knew what it was to have a truly terrible parent, and my dad was not one of them. He was a good guy who worked hard and loved me dearly. Now that I am out of the house, he dove into more projects at work and was even talking about traveling a little more.

"Hmm, looks a little busy. You run ahead and give our names while I park."

Half an hour later, my stomach was eating itself until we finally got seated in a leather booth by a window. We ordered our food the second the server came over to greet us and my dad laughed at me. "Did you skip eating for two days to prepare for this meal?"

"You know it! I gotta make the best of it when I'm offered a free meal." There was a time we would never have joked about eating. Hell, there was a stretch of time when both of us avoided talk of food and both avoided eye contact as full plates of food got pushed aside.

"So, how are your classes going?" Here it comes. I'm actually a little surprised it took him so long to get to his questionnaire.

"They are great. I've made a few friends, I've done well on all the assignments so far. There was a paper I was struggling with for Psych, but I hunkered down and finally got it done."

"Any guys catch your eye? We can find them when I drop you off, and I can give them all a strict warning."

I smiled despite myself. I knew well that my dad had a very different high school career than I did. The football star that was always surrounded by friends, and a different girl on his arm in every picture I saw of him. Then, he met my mom and fell in love. It seemed like once she caught his attention, every other aspect of his life fell away so all his attention could center on her. I had exactly one boyfriend in eleventh grade, who promptly dumped me when my weight spiked up once more. His dumping promptly led me to start purging again, and at the beginning of my senior year, I actually had to be hospitalized as my body struggled to get the proper nutrients.

I didn't exactly fit in. Few people wanted to be friends with the eating-disorder girl with the boring older dad.

"Not much to tell on that front. There is a guy in my Psych class, Logan, he's majoring in Criminal Justice. He's nice, but I don't think he's really interested. I think most guys are in a committed relationship or playing the field."

"Was Logan at the party you went to?" The server returned with our plates and they saved me from answering for a minute. The smell of fried food instantly sent my stomach into a hunger frenzy. Before, Brittany's comment about my weight gain would have truly damaged me. But after I was hospitalized and saw what it did to my father, I stopped looking at my body like some grotesque statue that should be destroyed. I tried to look at myself as a daughter who was loved. It helped. So did a lot of therapy. I still struggled a lot, but anytime I felt the urge to run off to the bathroom, I just thought back to the haggard expression of my father sitting by my bed in the hospital. He'd been through too much. We both had.

"He was. It was actually him and some of his friends throwing the party." I shrugged and took a bite of fried cheese. I ignored his patient gaze, knowing he would demand more information. I ate another mozzarella stick before I finally gave in and looked up.

"And just how was your first college party?"

"Dad, you know you can trust me. I didn't drink or do anything stupid. In fact, my roommate did all the drinking and stupid things, and I just made sure she got home okay. Then Brittany, from high school, tried to cause some drama, but it was taken care of."

"I'm sorry sweetheart, I don't want to be that parent. I just worry about you. We have a terrible history with alcohol, and I know you are in college and should enjoy some different experiences, but drinking always makes me nervous. And I guess while we are on sore subjects, have you been going to your support group? You look great, healthy."

"Yes, see, I'm eating." I took a huge bite and smiled as much as I could with my mouth stuffed with food. "And usually it's much healthier food I'm eating too, though I have my fair share of pizza and tacos." I actually hadn't been to the eating disorder support group in a few weeks, but that was just because I felt fine and school was getting in the way. I actually made sure Wednesday was a free day so I could study and go to the group, but that quickly turned into studying, writing papers, and sleeping instead.

"Okay, good. I'll stop with the third degree now." He held up his hands and smiled at me before digging into his burger. We talked about a project he was trying to land at work, and I told him more about my classes. As soon as I started to get full, I pushed my plate aside. As much as Brittany wanted to comment on my weight, I'd come a long way. Before, I would overeat until I had to throw up. Slowly, *finally*, I was coming to a place where I finally felt a truce with food.

"Well, I guess I should start getting you back. I know

you have schoolwork to get to and you are just being kind to dear old dad."

"Of course not, Dad. I miss you too, you know. It's weird. All these years it's just been the two of us, and now I'm in a dorm that is never quiet, with a roommate that spends far too much time worrying about what I'm wearing before I leave the room." He gave a spurt of laughter as he paid the bill and led me out, carrying my box of leftovers for me. "You were wonderful. You never bugged me about my clothes."

"Maybe I should have cared a little more, though. I mean-" He looked down at his lap after buckling his seatbelt. I knew what was coming, and I wished he would just look up, smile, and drive. "You should have had a mother around to help you with all that. I wasn't there for you, not in the way you really needed. It took me much longer to realize you were having trouble than it should have, you know. I never should have let you fall that far. I should ha-"

"Dad, stop. None of that is your fault. Mom refused help, and she made her choices. It is what it is. I went through some stuff and didn't know how to deal with it properly. That's not your fault. You got me help and I'm better now, okay? I'm in college, I have friends, and a guy to moon over from afar. I'm exactly as I should be." I reached over and took his hand in mine. His fingers engulfed mine and wrapped me in a feeling of safety. There was something calming about him. Maybe it had to do with the fact that he and my mother waited so long before having me. I knew they believed they couldn't have children, and then at forty-two he got a little surprise from my mother.

He drove me back to the dorm, and I leaned back in my seat. The mother I knew was a completely different woman from the one he had loved. After the...incident, he packed away all of her pictures, got rid of everything that was hers. He worked to erase her and her memories from our lives. When I was fourteen, though, I found the boxes of pictures, the cards they had exchanged over their twenty years of marriage, and nothing about it computed with all the memories I had of her.

In the pictures, her hair had a brilliant sheen, as though she brushed it a thousand times a day. Her smile lit up the room, reaching her eyes and warming them like melted chocolate. My father held her in a possessive manner I never witnessed in real life. Like she was something precious that needed to be protected and worshiped. The woman I knew, however...memories flashed through my mind in a way that made me feel sick. The smell of sickness that hung on her clothes, how her breath smelled like alcohol, her teeth unbrushed and her hair knotted and sticking out in odd angles.

I didn't remember love; my memories were of fighting, voices raised and hysterical crying that would always reach me, even if I had my head stuffed under a pillow. I don't know when exactly the change happened to her, but the pictures I saw made it clear it had something to do with me. Maybe she hadn't wanted me, maybe she suffered from postpartum and it was never recognized and treated...

"Are you okay, sweetheart?"

"Yeah, just thinking about a paper I should start on. Sorry. I always get a little sleepy after eating." The smiles in her pictures suddenly seemed forced as she held me as an infant. My father's smiles got even bigger in the early pictures. There was pride there, pure joy, but my mother looked like I had sucked all the happiness from her.

I knew it was something I shouldn't spend my time thinking about. But one had to wonder what could have changed her so much. How could a little baby make her life so terrible that she started drinking and throwing everything she loved away? That she could-

I reached over and turned up the radio. I needed to burn away my thoughts, drown out the next memories before they took over and had me crumbling. My dad didn't need that. He would only blame himself, and he didn't deserve that. He glanced sideways at me, but I just stared ahead and really started thinking about the paper I needed to write. Hell, I'd think about Brittany if it would keep thoughts of my mother away.

CHAPTER 4

"Hey stranger." Logan grabbed my arm after class and tugged me to a stop. It was almost two weeks since he talked to Brittany for me and got the pictures taken down. "You know, I was kind of waiting for you to approach me. Call me a hero, offer me a meal for my great deed of dealing with Brittany, but you've kind of left me hanging. We talked for like two minutes on the phone when I told you I got her to take them down and that was it. Not even a spare text to make sure I wasn't damaged." He put a hand to his chest and made a look of pure hurt.

"Well, you seem to have escaped unscathed from what I can see." I took my time perusing him, just to make sure.

"Was she awful?"

"You can't see the emotional toll." Logan ran his fingers through his hair before shaking his head and frowning down at me. "Woman, what do I have to do to get you to buy me a thank you meal? We are taking Psychology. I can pour my heart out to you, tell you all my traumas-"

"Oh, my goodness." Laughter burst from me before I could stop it. "Fine, I'll get you some food! I'm free now. What do you want?" He regarded me for a moment, his eyes serious before frowning.

"No, you know what? I'm going to take you on a date instead. You're single, right? No one is going to jump me if I feed you and flirt a little?"

"What?" My smile slipped from my face.

"Autumn," He spoke slower, patiently while my brain turned to cotton. "Would you like to go on a date with me?"

"Right now?" I looked down at my clothes: scuffed sneakers, jeans, and a baggy sweatshirt with the Eiffel Tower. Not exactly date material. Oh god, what had Ava done to me?

"Well, you're hungry, right?" I nodded silently and before I knew it, he had my bag off my arm and over his own, then his hand took mine and he started leading me away. Actually, I was anything but hungry. I tried to eat snacks throughout the day rather than actual meals. It kept me from getting queasy. After everything I put my body through, I no longer digested food very well. I certainly would not say all that to him, though. I could eat something, anything, to spend some time with him. My skin was on fire where it touched him.

"So, I've hardly talked to you since the party. Anything new?"

"Not really. I saw my dad the other day for lunch. I'm actually ahead of work for my classes at the moment, though I have a statistics test coming up that I'm not looking forward to. Math was never my strong suit." My mouth moved and words came out. They seemed normal enough, but I solely placed my focus on where our palms touched.

"Hmm, wish I could help you there, but I'm afraid I'm in the same boat. I have a test coming up on the American court system. There are so many names and dates to remember."

His thumb brushed over my palm as we walked, and I wondered when I died and entered my own personal heaven. Though I suppose if I had died, I would no longer have to take math tests. "Hope you don't mind if we don't go anywhere fancy. I decided on this at the last minute. I mean, I waited two weeks for you to call me, after all."

"Man, she must have worked a number on you, huh? You aren't about to let this go."

"You make yourself some fine enemies, let me tell you." We went into a small pizza joint, and he led us to a corner table and handed me a menu. "Now, we can split a pizza if you don't like any weird toppings, but they also make great subs here."

"What constitutes weird? Because I'm really into anchovy and pineapple pizza." I kissed my fingers and did my best Italian accent, which would bring shame to me if anyone who was actually Italian heard it.

"Ugh, I changed my mind. I no longer desire to date you."

"Okay, so this is really a date? Not just a 'I helped a girl out, so now I want to give her a hard time'?"

"Could you shorten the title a little there? Jeez, take a breath. And yes, *I* asked you on a date if you recall."

"Okay, fine then." I rested my arms on the table and looked him dead in the eyes, dark blue and forever dancing with mirth. "How did you get Brittany to take everything down? And why do you know where her dorm is?" Did you kiss her? Do you find her attractive?

"Well, I know where her dorm is because she texted me where it was after the party, you know, in case I changed my mind. And I got her to agree to take it down by, I'm ashamed to say, calling her some very unflattering things and then threatening to go to her dorm RA and tell them she was also drinking underage and was harassing a friend of mine. So seriously, what are your topping choices?"

"Mushrooms or pepperoni."

"How about both?" He wiggled his eyebrows and jumped up to place our order at the counter. When he sat back down, he looked me over. "So it's my turn. What is your father's name?"

"Jack, he runs a construction company."

"Jack Crowe, awesome name. He should write dark poetry like Poe or something with a name like that. How about your mother?"

It felt like a hand squeezed around my heart, but I forced out the words, trying to look nonchalant. "Leah, but she died when I was seven."

"Wow, I'm sorry to hear that. Are you close with your dad, though?"

"Yeah." I let out a little sigh of relief that he didn't dig more into that information. "What about your family?"

"My dad, Michael, is a cop, coming from a long line of cops. My mother, Angela, is a middle school teacher, English and History. I come from a long line of math haters."

"And you want to be a police officer, too?"

"Yeah, I've always wanted to help people. And in this day and age, I feel like we need some more good cops on the force, you know? I think too many cops forget they are supposed to be there to serve the community and want to just throw their weight around. Everywhere you go there are people looking down on others for whatever lame ass reason, but when a cop does it...I feel like it's worse, you know?" At my silence he waved a hand, "Sorry, just every day there is something else on the news about a cop not doing their job right and it gives everyone else a bad name. My father has been on the force for twenty-plus years, and he drags himself home after a tough day, his eyes bloodshot, his back stiff...He goes out every day and tries to help people and he's demonized because other cops are asses."

"No, you're right, and I think it's good you're passionate about the work you want to do."

"And you, a Psych major. You clearly want to help people, too."

"Yeah." I shrugged. It was hard to explain my professional choice without going into my childhood, which I had no desire to do. Not on a first date, and hopefully never. He drummed his knuckles on the table when I didn't add more, but then our pizza and drinks arrived, and he seemed to forget the conversation as they presented food to his apparently empty stomach.

"Where have you been all day? I got back from class and you weren't here. Usually by the time I'm done, you're holed up in your little corner. I thought you might have been kidnapped or something."

"Ha, Ha, though I kinda was." I let that stew for a minute before I plopped down on my bed and leaned my back against the wall. "Logan caught me after class and took me on an impromptu date."

"What?" Her voice rose an octave and her eyes seemed to bulge from her head. I told her about it, and told her he invited me to go with him and some friends to an amusement park before it closed down for the season.

"After that, he walked me back to our building, and he kissed me."

"What!" Ava jumped from her chair and stood gaping

at me.

"Just a quick little kiss on the lips, then he squeezed my hand and sent me up." I watched her jump up and down, barely able to stop myself from joining. He actually kissed me. I thought I was in love with him from the moment he walked by me to sit in the back of our shared class, but now...Now I realized I was really in danger.

"I want every detail!"

"There really isn't more to tell. Next week, we are going to drive up to the park and meet a few of his friends there."

She frowned. "Did you tell him you don't really do rides?"

"Yes, he said if I didn't mind waiting while he got on a coaster or two, he would ride the teacups with me for the rest of the day." I stuck my tongue out at her. The day after we met, she dragged me to the park as a "roommate bonding experience." Two seconds into arriving, she was annoyed with me because I told her I'd hold her bag while she and Riley got on the log flume. I never understood why people got so offended by the fact that I didn't enjoy the feeling of having my stomach twist and turn, and I've never been one to stop anyone else from having a good time...

"Are you sure you gave him a clear picture? He may think he can talk you into it."

"Ava, get over it. It will be fine!"

"Well, I guess we should put off plans for your birthday, then." She had planned on taking me out for my birthday, which would be the day after our trip. Since her plans probably involved me getting drunk, I wasn't that upset about her putting it off. "Are you going to hang out at all before then?"

"Probably. We talked about getting together to study."

"Ohhh, I'm going to pick a few outfit options for you!" I knew it would be a fight I couldn't win, so I just sat back and appreciated knowing I wouldn't have to worry about what to wear. Which gave me more time to think about that kiss.

CHAPTER 5

Logan shifted his car into park, and I almost cried. I didn't want the car ride to end. We spent most of the last week together. Usually just studying together during our spare time, but still, together. But this little outing was different. We weren't on campus or talking about school; we were just holding hands, fighting over the radio. Logan kept singing all the girl power songs that came on at the top of his lungs, while I recorded him on my phone in case I ever needed to blackmail him in the future.

"You know, I really think I like you, Autumn." He met my eyes after he parked, and squeezed my hand. "I'm glad you came today."

"Thanks for inviting me." He brushed a thumb over

my cheek and chills raced down my spine. I leaned into him, pressed my palms against his chest while he pulled me closer, taking my mouth with a new force. We had kissed a few times over the past week, but we were usually at the library or somewhere else public. This kiss was different. It demanded passion in a way that took my breath away. His fingers moved over my arms and goosebumps spread across my skin, making me more sensitive to everything. When his tongue slipped past my lips, I met him full on, and he groaned, pulling me tighter, nearly pulling me out of my seat. Everything changed in an instant. I almost crawled across the gearshift to sit on his lap.

His phone interrupted, playing a portion of *The Devil went Down to Georgia*, which made me giggle. He broke from our kiss and leaned back, ignoring his phone for another moment while he caught his breath. Then he flashed me a tempting grin and answered.

While he talked, I leaned back in my seat and gathered myself. I suddenly had no desire to go to the park, no desire to hang out with his friends. I wanted him to drive me somewhere where we could be alone and continue that kiss. My cheeks heated at the thought. A week with him and I was ready to take the next step, a step I had not taken before. But what will he think when he finds out I'm a virgin? Christ, what will he think if he finds out basically *anything* private about me? So far I'd been able to keep our conversations light but there was a lot of darkness in my past, in my mind, and it wouldn't exactly be fair to lay all that at his feet and ask him to take me. My baggage does not make for a light load.

"They beat us here and are waiting inside the gates. Are you ready?"

"Maybe one more kiss for the road?" I quirked an eyebrow and put on my best smile. Logan was quick to oblige.

"Happy early birthday, Autumn!" Riley stood with Jerry and Levi and shouted the greeting at me the moment I came into view. I cringed as heads turned toward me.

"I didn't know it was your birthday. Why didn't you say anything?" Logan looked as shocked as I felt.

"Well, I didn't exactly tell anyone. Ava found out, but I asked her not to say anything. Which, clearly, she ignored."

"When is it?"

"Tomorrow," I mumbled. I didn't like that he looked a little hurt at my answer. Trying to play it off, I gave a small shrug. "I just don't really celebrate my birthday. My dad and I would always just kind of hang out, get a grocery store cake, and watch a movie. It's really not a big deal."

"Try telling that to Ava." Riley bumped my arm. "She is dying to take you out now that you'll be legal."

"I think Ava should stay away from alcohol for a while, plus *she's* not legal."

"Yeah, but her roommate can now supply." Riley gave me a pointed look, and the idea of my birthday seemed even less appealing than before. From the sound of it, I would have some arguments in my future.

"So," Jerry, Logan's very fit roommate, seemed oblivious to any tension. "What should we ride first?"

"Where's Alice?" Logan asked, his gaze finally tearing away from me.

"Ran to the bathroom. I'll just text her where we are going." Everyone decided on the coaster that was just inside the entrance, since we were already close. Logan finally took my hand again, so I leaned into him as we all got into the very long line. "I'm sorry I didn't tell you. I didn't mean to hurt your feelings. I'm just really not into birthdays."

"Okay." He didn't quite meet my eyes, but then another woman joined our group. I assumed she was Alice, since she gave Jerry a kiss.

"You must be Autumn! Nice to meet you."

"You too." The line moved, and we were coming up to the gate. "Guess that's my cue to leave you guys for the rest of the wait. Does anyone want me to hold anything for them?"

"What?" Levi frowned at me from around Riley's head.

"Autumn doesn't like coasters," Logan answered for me.

Levi and Jerry both looked like they were missing out on some joke, but Riley knew the deal, so she just handed over her small purse and thanked me. Alice ended up handing over her wallet, and Jerry gave me his baseball cap.

"Have fun!" I gave a small wave and left the line. I was coming back around to stand near the coaster when I heard Levi scoff.

"Why did you bring her if she's not going to ride anything?"

"Did anyone hear her complaining about waiting for us to ride? She's not into coasters, it's not a big deal. It's not like she's trying to stop us from getting on," Logan snapped.

"Plus," Riley jumped in, "there is someone to hold our stuff. Less to worry about."

"I'm just saying, you couldn't find a girl that would actually be fun to hang out with? Plus, who's saying she didn't just run off with all of your stuff?"

"Levi! She's my friend." Riley slapped his arm.

"Yeah, and my girlfriend. If you have a problem with that, then maybe we should step out of the line too." 'Girlfriend' snagged my attention. We hadn't stated out loud if we were officially an item or not, even after spending most of the week together stealing kisses in quiet moments. But to hear him say it to his friend took my breath away.

"Whatever man." I stepped away before anyone saw I was within hearing range. It felt good to know both Riley and Logan were willing to stand up for me, though I really didn't understand what the big deal was. I sat on a bench and watched the coaster whizz past me. Just the thought of my stomach turning and free-falling made me want to curl up in a ball under a pile of heavy blankets. Levi was probably right, I'm not much fun to hang out with, and he wasn't the first person to say so about me. I don't drink, eating with me can be a nightmare, and I don't really like rides... But I liked Logan and, despite my flaws, he seemed to like me. Of course, he didn't really *know* my flaws.

It was their turn to get on, so I watched the coaster as

it went through the ride. Just as they were about to go through a loop someone sat beside me. "You are mine, Autumn."

Startled, and expecting to find someone I knew grinning at their joke, I turned toward the person but suddenly I was alone again on the bench. I jumped to my feet and looked around, searching for a familiar face. The coaster rode overhead, and I turned back toward it. My heart stopped. My mother was standing in front of me, her face haggard, blood dried around her nose and mouth, her eyes watching me with a blank stare. She reached out her hand toward me. My world tilted, and I thought I would faint. I took a step toward her, blinked, and she was gone.

"What the hell..." I looked around again, but I was standing alone under the coaster, a few steps away from the bench. I could hear my heart pounding in my ears and I felt weak as all the adrenaline left my body, so I moved quickly to sit at the bench again. Everyone kept moving as though nothing odd happened and after a few breaths, I finally felt more in control of myself. Clearly, I let my mind play tricks on me somehow. It was probably just the stress of my birthday.

The ride ended, so I moved to stand at the exit. "How

was it?" I put on an extra cheery smile and looked directly at Levi as he and Riley stepped out first. I handed Riley back her bag as Levi answered it was fun, but kept his gaze just over my head. When Logan came out, he smiled at me, his face flushed from the ride, and I truly grinned. He took my hand and everything seemed right with the world once more.

"Okay, I want to get on the swings!" Alice pointed and jumped up and down like a small child, which made everyone laugh.

"Hmm, I think I'd like to skip that one." Logan glanced down at me. "I kind of want to ride the viewing tower. I know you guys always say it's lame, but I like it. If you don't mind missing out on the swings?" He rubbed a thumb over my wrist and I felt a silent conversation pass between us. He wanted to be alone with me as much as I wanted to be alone with him. I nodded and leaned into him as we parted ways with the rest of the group.

The ride was an enormous tower that had viewing "pods". Each pod sat two people, and it was basically a bench while the entire front was a window. We sat down and the ride attendant closed us in. "Sorry if you really like the swings. I just always liked this and everyone else thinks it's lame."

"No, it's nice." I leaned against his side, and he reached an arm around me, pulling me tight against him. It felt right. The ride started, and we slowly lifted off the ground. The pod would rise and slowly turn so you got a full view of the park and the land surrounding it. But I wasn't looking out the window. Logan's lips pressed against mine, and I was lost. Lost in the scent that was uniquely his, the warmth of his touch, the feel of his teeth scraping against my bottom lip.

A sound escaped from my throat and the grip he had on me tightened at the sound. He sucked on my bottom lip and my body erupted like it was hit by lightning. I fell into him as he kissed me deeper. His hand slipped under the hem of my shirt, resting so his thumb brushed the bottom of my ribs. I was on fire and didn't care. I was wondering how much we could get away with up here, my hand splayed across his chest and thinking about wandering lower, when he pulled back with a small growl and rested his forehead against mine.

"Can we stay up here forever?" I sighed, sharing his air and already missing his lips.

"I think I could live with that. Though, down there they have funnel cake..." He weighed his hands in front of him like he was trying to decide.

"Wow, choosing funnel cake over kissing me. You

know how to make a girl feel good."

"Yes, but I like to believe I can have it all. We could have funnel cake and make out."

"I don't know. That sounds too easy. If we all just went around trying to be happy and have it all, what would come of this world?"

"A lot of happy fat people. Which I gotta say, sounds like a world I want to live in." He grinned and flashed me a wink.

"It does sound nice." I leaned forward, for once feeling fearless, and pressed my hands against the glass, looking down at the dots of people below us. Suddenly, the small circling pod jolted to a stop and the door I was leaning on became unhinged and sprang open.

"Shit!" Logan grabbed the back of my shirt and yanked me against him. Screams erupted around us as everyone else dealt with the fact we were stopped hundreds of feet in the air without being strapped in. The only thing protecting us from falling to our deaths was a door that was now unhatched and open. "Oh, my god...oh my god. I could have fallen! What the hell just happened?" The fact that I was about two seconds away from falling to my death hit me in one sudden punch that made me feel off kilter. Everything spiraled in my mind, sending me through the years as panic seized me.

"It's okay, shh," He pulled me against him and rested my head against his chest. As calmly as he was speaking, his heart was racing. "Something must have gone wrong with the ride. The safest ride in the park and it breaks down...I guess I was wrong about having everything."

I knew he was trying to joke around, calm me down, but it wasn't working. Flashes of standing on a bridge were taking over my vision, blocking out everything else. Only a minute ago I was having the time of my life, kissing a guy I like, actually enjoying the heights. But now I just felt the wind hitting my cheek, whipping my hair around.

"Are you crying? Autumn, we'll be okay. We just have to sit back in our seats until they get everything moving again. It's okay, I promise." I heard his voice, heard his words, but tears started streaming down my cheeks and I could feel my body shaking. It became violent and uncontrollable. I couldn't breathe. My chest had something heavy resting on it and I couldn't draw in oxygen. It took me a moment to realize the strange wheezing sound I was hearing was coming from me.

"Shit! Autumn, you have to calm down. You're going

into shock or something right now. Look at me, don't look down. Just look at me." His large, warm hand touched my cheek and forced me to meet his gaze. His face swam in front of me and instead of his face, I saw my mother's.

"I have to save your soul, honey. This is the only way. I love you so much. It will be over quickly, I promise. We are going to fly. You want to fly, don't you?"

"No, I can't!" I pushed away from him and put my head between my knees. He tried to talk again, but I covered my ears; I needed to block it all out. His voice kept blending with my mother's and the flashes of memory were taking over my vision. "I can't be up here...I can't...We need to get down. We need to get down now! I want to go home." My voice sounded raspy as I still struggled to get enough air and sobs were tearing from me.

"Autumn, please...are you afraid of heights?" He started rubbing my back but the soft touch felt like claws raking down my skin. I carefully avoided looking down and met his eyes. His blue eyes. I concentrated hard on them. They were deep blue, but grew lighter around the edges. Usually they were light with laughter, but right now his gaze was serious, squinting in concern.

"There is so much, *so much* you don't know." The

words spilled out in a rush and I thought my heart might burst free from my chest. It was pounding so quickly. "I can't do this...I can't...I'm so messed up, but I felt normal with you. But now-" I broke off and almost looked down. At the last second, I looked at my lap instead.

"What in the world are you talking about? It's okay to be afraid, you almost fell. It's okay."

It's not okay, it's not okay, nothing is okay. "No...tomorrow is my birthday..." The tears started again. I lied earlier about my father and I just getting a store cake and watching movies together for my birthday. We pretended my birthday didn't exist. We didn't talk about it, we avoided each other. I usually spent it holed up in my room with a book or something until the day ended. I'd already thought of ways out of going anywhere with Ava the moment she found out when my birthday was. "My mother...she died..." I pressed my palms on my eyes.

"Your mother died on your birthday? I'm so sorry, Autumn. Shit." He reached for my hand, but I yanked back. I couldn't let him touch me. Not with everything on the surface. I needed the ground. I needed a heavy blanket to hide under. But I couldn't have him, not when I was like this, probably never. I was too easy to break. I'd been broken and put back together too many times.

"She didn't die, she jumped."

We are going to fly. Don't you want to fly?

He let out a hiss and gripped my hand. "I have you, Autumn." The words were simple, and he meant them. I needed to purge myself of the story, it was just sitting there at the top and I needed to get rid of it. I needed to keep looking at him and only him. If I looked around at how high we were the panic would win.

"I was with her. She was drunk, and my dad tried to stop her, but she took me. I was seven, it was my birthday. It was my birthday." I had to force the words through my constricted throat.

"It's okay; you don't have to talk right now." He pulled me back against his chest as the shaking started again. I couldn't tell if it was just me shaking, or if he was now, too. Maybe he wanted me to stop telling him the story. It was a terrible one and maybe he didn't want that burden. But I needed it off my chest right now. I would tell him, and if he decided it was too much, then we could part ways. At that moment, I wasn't even sure I would survive. It seemed like perfect poetry for me to die the day before my birthday, falling from some great height.

"She told me she was trying to save me. I was so scared, Logan. I just wanted to go home. I was supposed to have friends over for a party and cake and I was afraid I'd miss it. My mom was going on and on about my soul, and flying, and how she had to do it, and I just wanted to go home. I just wanted my dad and my friends."

"Autumn..." His voice was quiet now as he stroked my hair. No one had ever stroked my hair before.

"She picked me up and held me. She kissed my forehead...and she jumped. My mother jumped off a bridge to kill me."

CHAPTER 6

We sat in the pod surrounded by silence. I was drained. I wanted nothing more than to get away from Logan and hide under the covers for the rest of the year. He didn't seem too concerned with my silence and didn't attempt to get me to talk. It took them three hours to get us down from the ride. I spent those three hours in a near panic, switching between the present and the horrible memories of my past. He did his best to keep me calm. Logan didn't ask questions about the story I'd told; he let me cry against his shoulder, and he held me close to help me feel safe.

He stroked my hair and talked to me. He even just started going down all the cases he was currently studying just to pass the time, and keep my mind in the present. But the second our feet finally hit the ground, we broke apart. He caught up with his friends while Riley hugged me and gave me a soda and a bag of popcorn.

As soon as he reassured everyone we were okay, he grabbed my arm and told me he was taking me home. The park let us know they were going to refund our money, and they gave us vouchers for season passes for next year, but I had a feeling I would just give mine to Ava and call it quits.

We were halfway to the campus when he sighed and glanced my way. "So, that date went exactly as planned. Clowns were supposed to jump out at us too in the parking lot, but I guess they forgot my deposit."

"I'm sorry, Logan." I still felt numb, but I could also feel loss. For a moment I'd had him, I'd been his, but the second that ride broke, that had all come crashing to an end. "You were really great up there. I'm a mess. It's not a big deal. I know you want out of this, and I don't blame you. A college guy should not have to worry about the crazy girl he asked on a date."

"Autumn, please shut up." Startled, I looked back at him. "You had a very tough day, and tomorrow is obviously not your favorite day of the year. That doesn't make you crazy. You've had horrible things happen to you and you are still standing. That definitely doesn't make you crazy, that makes you strong. Now, I'd like to ask you to stay at my place tonight? I'm okay if you say no, but I think we could get some sandwiches, put away all study material, and spend the night watching movies together huddled under blankets. After being dangled in the air with a cool wind hitting me for three hours, I almost feel like I won't be warm again."

"How are you possibly asking me to stay over at your place for the night after the day we had and everything I told you?"

"Don't worry, I plan on being a complete gentleman. However, especially after your little speech, I feel like if I let you go back to your dorm, I won't see you again. I don't want you to push me away, Autumn. What do you say?"

"I also have an eating disorder. I spent my entire highschool career dangerously dropping weight only to overeat myself into two sizes bigger than I am right now. Logan, I'm not still standing. I'm hanging on by a thread. As you saw clearly today, the smallest thing will set me off and send me spiraling."

He only paused for a moment before asking dryly, "so is that a no to sandwiches?"

"You are mine, Autumn." The voice came at me from the

darkness. The bridge hung above me and pain wracked my body. When I looked down, I saw my bone sticking through my skin, and I was seven years old again, crying at the edge of the stream. My mother's body lay crumpled beside me, her bones twisted at odd angles. I was crying out for help, moving in and out of consciousness. Then a hand reached out and grabbed my arm.

"I just wanted to save your soul." My mother talked through a twisted jaw and I screamed, desperate to get away-

"Autumn! Hey, you were dreaming. It's okay!" I jerked awake and strong arms came around me. I pushed away and ran for the bathroom. The images were still clear in my mind's eye, the mix of actual memories and a horrible nightmare. Logan's house was empty other than us. Levi and Jerry both stayed with their girlfriends. Logan and I spent the last few hours watching movies, talking about everything from my struggles to his funny anecdotes about his mother being his teacher for two years. The nightmare was still too fresh for me to leave his bathroom again to face him. It wasn't really a nightmare, it was a memory, and with it came roiling nausea that took all my power to fight against.

I ran cool water and patted my face and neck until I felt more settled. When I went back, Logan waited for me on the bed. "Happy birthday, Autumn. What would you like to do today?" He didn't mention anything about the nightmare, or me hiding in his bathroom. He just smiled in an easy way that was all his own.

"Oh, well, I have classes today, so, going to those." He caught my hand and pulled me onto the bed, tugging me beside him, and I was snuggling in before I could argue with myself. He kept his word about being a gentleman the night before. Other than some kissing, he kept his hands to himself and seemed content to snuggle.

"Skip with me today. Yesterday was not the fun filled day I planned. Let's have a re-do."

"I know we have season passes and all, but I don't think I'm really up for going back there just yet."

He chuckled and kissed my hair. "Not the park again. But something."

"I'd like that, really, but I need to go to class. I need all the points I can get for my statistics course. I had a really nice time last night though. Maybe we can get together tonight?"

"Ah, I have work tonight. You are working at the library tomorrow, right? I can stop by after my classes and then we can hang out?"

"Sounds perfect." I kissed him and instantly regretted it. Every part of me wanted to stay right there, in his arms, in this bed, all day. Skipping class and spending the day with him felt like celebrating a day I'd rather sleep through, though. The last thing I wanted to do was acknowledge my birthday, even if doing so meant more time with Logan.

So, I pulled myself together, and I stole his shower for a quick wash and ran out, needing to go back to my dorm to get my stuff for class. Luckily Ava had already left for her class, so I didn't have a list of questions to answer. I grabbed my backpack and unlocked my bike. I made it to my lecture just as the professor got started. He hardly glanced my way as I ran into the room and plopped myself down into my seat near the back.

I did my best to follow along and take notes, but math always seemed to hang over my head, just out of reach. My mind was drifting when I glanced toward the corner of the room and saw a man that wasn't there before. He had a black hat pulled down and his face angled so I couldn't see it.

The rest of the room seemed to fade as the shadowed face turned toward me. "Come with me, Autumn. You are destined to be mine." He rose and approached slowly. I tried to cringe away, but I seemed frozen in place. He held out a hand to me, and suddenly we were alone. "Autumn." His hand brushed my cheek, and I cringed away, standing up from my desk to get away. I wasn't sure how the class emptied so quickly without my noticing, but I didn't like being left alone with this man who seemed to know me.

"Who are you? How do you know my name?"

"You have been mine since before you were conceived. I have waited all these years for you. Come with me, now." His voice was impossibly deep and made me feel tired.

"No, I don't know you..." I backed away, but he made no move to grab me. I made my escape and fled from the room. Vaguely, I realized someone was calling my name, but I needed to get away from the room before the man started talking to me again. Just his body being close to me made my skin crawl.

I turned the corner and nearly walked into someone. A hand reached out and grabbed my arm, catching me before I could fall, and I looked into my mother's face. I froze in fear and opened my mouth in a silent scream. "Happy birthday, baby girl."

"Autumn, come with us. It's where you belong." The man tried to grab me from behind, but I came back to myself. I jerked my arm free from my mother's grasp, ignoring the sharp pain it caused, and ran. I was probably missing my next class, but it didn't matter. The only thing that mattered was getting away. By the time I reached my dorm, I was out of breath. My bag hung off my elbows, and I dropped it to the ground, not caring if my laptop broke into a million pieces. I struggled for breath, my body shaking, my skin clammy, and realized I left my bike in front of the lecture hall.

My stomach rolled, and I made it to the trash can just in time. I hadn't had time to eat breakfast, so I mostly dry heaved until my stomach and throat were raw. In a daze, I crawled into bed and pulled the covers up to my chin and drifted into a dreamless sleep.

"Autumn, what happened? Tracy called me to say you just got up and walked out of your statistics class this morning. Autumn?" Ava's voice found me through a haze in my mind, but I couldn't get myself to move. I wasn't sure how long I had been lying there, but I knew I must have missed my classes for the day. I couldn't find it in me to care.

"Autumn?" She placed freezing fingers on my forehead and I cringed away with a whimper. I just wanted my birthday to be over so I could stop seeing these horrible visions of my mother. Stress must be getting to me, and my mind was dealing with it by bringing me visions of her.

Some time passed with the sounds of Ava moving around the dorm room. She didn't talk to me again for a while and I sank back into some space between consciousness and sleep. Then she was shaking me and nearly pulling me into a sitting position. Her eyes were glazed with worry. She was saying something to me, but there was a buzzing in my ears blocking out her words.

I blinked through the haze covering my eyes and realized she was handing me a bowl of soup. "Eat this, Autumn."

More time passed, then I could hear Ava mumbling something, but her words made little sense. I got sick two more times, and she plied me with crackers and more soup, but every drop made my stomach protest. I saw another flash of the man in the hat. He stood at the corner of our dorm room but then he looked at Ava and walked out the door. I felt dizzy and weak so I laid back down. Restless sleep found me once more.

I woke up feeling worse. My stomach seemed to beg for food, but just the thought made my head spin. I pressed my eyes shut and heard two voices.

"We were supposed to meet at the library, but they

said she hadn't come in."

"Yeah, I called them to tell them she was sick. She hasn't gotten out of bed since yesterday morning."

"Has she eaten anything?"

"I tried, but she kept getting sick. I think she's running a fever, but when I tried to give her some meds she just got sick and I wanted her to at least stay hydrated. If she was like this again tomorrow, I was going to call her dad and make him take her to the doctor."

A weight joined me on the bed, settling down behind me so my body rolled in that direction. Cool fingers touched my forehead again and brushed the hair from my face. "Hey there, Autumn. I thought you said you didn't want to miss any classes? But it turns out, you didn't want to spend the day in bed with me, you wanted to spend it in bed alone and sick. My feelings are hurt."

"Logan?" My throat was raw and my voice cracked. I tried to sit up, but my vision swam and he gripped my shoulders.

"Yeah, apparently you think being sick is a good excuse to blow me off. Little do you know, I have a great immune system, and now you're stuck with me." I couldn't find it in me to argue, so I just settled back against the pillow.

I must have drifted off a little because the feel of him settling in next to me once more drew me from rest. The TV was on and he helped me sit up and adjust the pillows behind my back. "Buttered toast and chicken noodle soup. My specialty." My stomach rolled when I took a bite. I paused and breathed deep, trying to concentrate on the sound of the comedy show he turned on.

"You don't need to stay. I must look terrible if I look half as bad as I feel."

"It's not your highest point, I'll admit, but I plan on being a police officer, so I should probably get used to people who aren't looking their best." He grinned at me. I wanted to punch his arm, but it would take too much movement, so I stayed put. I brought the spoon to my mouth and even the small sip of soup warmed my whole body. I ate slowly, but Logan seemed to sense that I was struggling. The entire time I worked on eating, he kept up a distracting conversation and rubbed my back in soothing circles. Finally, I cleaned my bowl and ate two pieces of toast.

"That's my girl." He kissed my temple and chucked my chin. "How are you feeling now?"

"A little better. Food definitely helped."

"What happened? You seemed fine when you left

yesterday." Ava had left us at some point, and I took a moment to truly look around the dorm. It was Friday now, and from the lighting out the window, it was almost over. I had missed two days worth of classes, and my shift at the library. From the looks of things, Ava had stayed in the dorm with me today. I vaguely remembered flashes of her plying me with food and me getting sick over and over every time I tried to eat. She must have skipped all her classes to take care of me.

"I don't really remember...I was sitting in class and I must have drifted off or something because I woke up and I was alone..." Logan gave me an odd look. "What?" I asked. I already decided I would not tell him about the hallucinations I had. Clearly I had just been coming down with something and my stress got the better of me.

"Ava said she got a text that you just walked out in the middle of your class." I tried to place what he was saying into my memory. It was one thing to hallucinate some man in the room, it was another thing to hallucinate away a room full of people and replace them with some creeper in a hat. "It's okay, go on."

"I...I just wasn't feeling well, so I came here. I was so out of it I left my bike at the lecture hall. It's probably been stolen by now."

"Hit you fast, huh?" He reached out and stroked my hair, tucking it back behind my shoulder. "Well, we'll let your stomach settle into that meal. Want to watch a movie or something?"

"It's Friday night, don't you have somewhere to go? I'm sure your friends are doing something."

"Trying to get rid of me? Here I am, trying to be a wonderful boyfriend and take care of my sick girlfriend, and you are trying to get rid of me."

"Not at all." I rested my head against his shoulder, wanting to just close my eyes again with his arms around me, but some human needs were calling to me. "It's just I haven't showered since the quick wash at your place and I also haven't brushed my teeth..."

"Can you make it to the bathroom okay? You haven't really eaten in two days either. You could wait until Ava gets back."

"I'll be okay, but you want to wait here while I shower?"

"Sure, I'll just use this magic box you have. It has moving pictures. Highly entertaining. You don't mind, do you?" I shook my head and moved carefully to stand. I felt weak, but I made it to my closet okay and pulled out my bathroom supplies and a change of clothes. When I caught sight of Logan, I found he was watching me with a worried expression, and I realized he had positioned himself so he could leap off the bed if he needed to get to me quickly.

"I'm okay. I'll be quick." It was a lie, though. The second the warm water hit me, I felt reinvigorated, and I showered much longer than I usually did. When I finally climbed out, dried off, and got dressed, I made my way to the other part of the bathroom so I could get to a sink and brush my teeth. Despite all the sleep, I had huge dark circles under my eyes and I looked like I lost five pounds in two days. My cheeks looked hollowed out, and horrible memories of making my body look like this on purpose, came back to me. I forced myself to look away and quickly brushed my teeth before returning to my dorm room.

I was relieved to find the room didn't smell like I had been getting sick for nearly forty-eight hours. Ava must have stayed on top of the trash pail. I was going to owe her big time.

"Here, you had some grapes in your fridge. We can munch on them while we watch a movie and then see how you are feeling after." Logan patted the spot beside him on my bed, but I motioned for him to get up. Now that I was feeling better, I wanted to strip the bed and put down new sheets and pillowcases. He helped me make the bed with my spare set and then jumped onto it, landing dead center, ruffling the blankets we just put down. "Ahhh, thanks, darling." He winked at me as he stretched his arms over his head, pulling his shirt just high enough to show a slash of skin above his waistband.

"Hey, move over!" He pouted and sat up, which sadly repositioned his shirt to cover himself again, but didn't move over. Instead, he propped a pillow behind his back before pulling me down. He positioned his legs on either side of me and wrapped his arms around me so my back was against his stomach, my head resting against him, surrounded by him. He kissed the top of my still wet hair and handed me the remote so I could find something to watch. I wasn't sure he could be any more perfect.

CHAPTER 7

"So, I ignored everything you said, and I planned on getting you a belated birthday present, but it got all screwed up."

"Serves you right for trying to do something birthday related for me." I had just gotten back from visiting my dad to find Logan waiting for me in front of my dorm building.

"Seriously though, look at this." He pulled his phone out of his pocket and started scrolling through pictures. "Every single one with you is messed up."

"Great, now I broke your camera with my ugly mug?"

He frowned at me. "Don't call my girlfriend ugly." He placed a gentle kiss on my cheek, which made my heart swell, then turned his phone to show me the pictures we took together over the past few weeks. One was from his party, just a quick shot while we had been talking in the room together. Apparently, one of his friends had taken his phone to take pictures of everyone. Another was a group shot a mother with her son took of all of us going into the amusement park sans Alice. There were a few selfies he took of us while we were on the viewing tower ride waiting to be rescued (he had a goofy face in every single one since he had been trying to calm me down and distract me). There was nothing unusual about the photos that I could see, but then he took out a small envelope and handed it over. Inside he had prints of each of the pictures and in every single one, something was wrong with my image. Either my face was blurred, there was a dark shadow over it, or it looked like a thin film was placed over me.

"They told me the image must have gotten damaged, but it looks fine on my phone. I'm sorry, I wanted to give you a book of pictures of us."

"Well, at least I have some great pics of you making funny faces now. I'll just cut my image out and paste you all over the walls. I'm sure Ava will enjoy that." He chuckled and kissed the tip of my nose. "I've got to run off to work, but I was hoping to catch you before I had to go."

"Right, so you could show me how my face broke your

camera...No wait, sorry, my face broke the whole printer, apparently."

"No, so I could give you this." He cradled my face and my heart came to life in my chest. His lips covered mine in tenderness, melting me until I was a puddle at his feet. It was hard to believe we've only been dating for a month. Everything with him seemed so natural and easy.

"Can I come over tonight?" I sighed when he pulled back. I hadn't planned on asking that, but I would be lying if I said I hadn't been thinking about it. His eyes darkened with desire. I had only stayed at his place the one time. In a month, we had yet to have sex, though I was sure he wanted it. But then he didn't answer right away. "I'm sorry. You had class this morning and you are going to work...You'll probably just want to crash tonight." I let go of his hand and took a step back. I had gotten so caught up in the kiss that I didn't consider that maybe he hadn't made a move in that direction because he didn't want to.

"No, it's not that. Trust me, I would give up a week's worth of sleep to spend more time with you. It's just that I told my parents I would come by for dinner tonight. My brother is in town so I wanted to see him."

"Oh! Why didn't you say something? That's great. We

have Psych together tomorrow, maybe we can grab lunch together after class, so you can tell me how it went?" I couldn't deny the relief that flooded through me. As strong as I like to think I've become, I find it discouraging how quickly my own thoughts and doubts can crowd my head.

"Why don't you come with me? Then you can sleep over and we can go to class together?"

"No, I wouldn't want to intrude. Besides, you can't just call your family and tell them last second you are bringing someone-"

"Well, I actually said I might bring you when I talked to my mother. I had planned on asking you to come, but then you said you made plans with your dad, and I had assumed it would be for dinner, so I didn't. Then yesterday you said it was breakfast, but I figured I would just let it be since it was last minute. But you're free and I'd like you to be there."

He sincerely wanted my company, but it wasn't the night I had in mind. Instead of holing up in his room for the night, I would be worried about how I looked and trying to eat in front of everyone, make small talk, and seem worthy to date their son....

"Stop," he put his hands on my shoulder, "I see your mind racing a hundred miles per minute. Just stop. Come with me. I want you there, and my family wants to meet you."

"Okay," I croaked, which earned a smile. The trouble I could get into, to earn a smile from him.

"Great, I'll text you when I get off work, and then I'll swing by and pick you up." He ducked down to kiss me once more, a soft pleasant kiss, and then he was jogging away. "Stop worrying!" He turned once, giving me a small wave. Easy for him to say.

When I started adding up all the favors I owed Ava, I no longer worried about my student loans. This girl was going to own my soul outright at the rate I was going. I needed to get some reading done for my classes, but I continued to stare at my closet, at the flowy dress she hung on the front. Before she ran off to meet Riley and some of her other friends, she helped me do a light makeover, doing my makeup and hair and then picked out the dress that cut just below my knees with a cinched waist. She'd picked it out for me when we went shopping together, but I hadn't worn it yet. After everything I'd put my body through, I was a terrible judge of how clothes fit me, but she said it just put the right curves on display without being gaudy. She was the fashion expert, after all, and I knew I couldn't be trusted with my view of my body.

Ava was a good friend. She could get on my nerves, and we were two very different people, but for the first time I really understood what it was to have a best friend. All growing up I was the odd girl out. People found out about what happened with my mother, how she leapt off a bridge while holding me. A story like that just doesn't go away. I got sad looks from parents and almost fearful glances from the other students.

My mother took the brunt of the fall, but my leg had a pretty bad break that took months to heal. After that, I had to go to rehab to get my muscles back in gear. It had been excruciating and the whole time I was confused and afraid. My mother had tried to kill me. Then she was dead. My dad could hardly look at me, I know now he blamed himself for letting her stay around even after the drinking started. He blamed himself that I almost died. And he truly lost the woman he loved. All those years with her drinking, losing her mind, and spewing crazy ramblings, he probably believed the woman from before was still there, and he could bring her back. But there was no coming back from the grave.

At the time, though, I believed my father blamed me. She died trying to get rid of me. My birth changed everything. And now he was stuck raising me by himself. It killed me that it took him close to a year to really look at me again. Every day, every hour, I died a little. It wasn't his fault; it was just the particular hand I was given. But those years of being the outcast wore on me. Soon I looked at myself like there was something ugly about me. It didn't take long for that to turn into an eating disorder, and a reason to cut. I never told anyone outside of therapy about the cutting, but I still have a few scars at the top of my thighs from it. There was a need to punish myself for whatever was wrong with me. I hold so much shame for the things I put my body through. It took a lot of therapy to even find a place where I could try to forgive myself, forget about trying to find time to forgive my mother.

Yet here I was. I was supposed to wear a pretty dress and meet my boyfriend's family. I was supposed to show them how I could deserve such a loving and *loved* person. There was no way I could do that. I didn't deserve him.

"You are right, you don't. You belong to me." A cracked voice spoke from the closet, and had me jolting out of my pity party. I was on my feet, my body rigid with fear.

"Who are you?" How did someone get in my room? How long had they been in here? A second later, the man with the hat stepped out from the closet and grinned at me. Sharp white teeth glinted at me from under the bridge of the hat.

"Your mother tried to end our deal, instead she forfeited her own soul. She thought she could get out of the blood oath. An oath that brought your parents years of happiness."

"What are you talking about? Get out! I'll scream!" I should be screaming now but my body seemed out of my control, the words barely above a whisper as I stood rigid in the middle of my room.

"Tut tut." He shook his head slowly, keeping his face tilted so the bridge of his hat blocked the view of it, and seemed to glide toward me. "You were right all those years ago. Each of those scars are the true image of who you are. You never should have been born, even your mother thought so."

"You aren't real," I covered my ears and sat back on the edge of my bed. "You can't be real. I'm going crazy."

"Come with me, Autumn. What a lovely name. Do you know why your mother chose that name for you? Your father didn't want to name you that, but your mother was insistent. Do you know why?" He was hovering over me, his voice clear as day even as I shoved fingers into my ears. I was really losing it. I thought before it was just stress from my birthday but now...was it because I was stressed about going to dinner? Was that my trigger? Haven't I dealt with enough for one lifetime? A crazy drunk mother who tried to kill me, a lifetime of self-loathing that I still haven't completely overcome...Now I had to lose my mind too! Was it genetic? Had my mother really been suffering all those years from some mental problem, and now I was getting it too?

"Oh God, oh God....help me..."

"God is not here, Autumn. You were born straight from a deal with a demon. Your soul had been forfeit since before conception. You. Are. Mine." He drew out the last word like it tasted good on his tongue.

My phone rang, and the man was gone. What. The. Hell. "Hello?" My voice was shaking, it grated against my throat to move the words past. My chest tightened with a breath that I couldn't quite draw. Logan didn't seem to notice anything odd, his voice cheerful on the other end. I stared into the closet across from me, waiting for something more to happen.

"Hey, I'm on my way. Going to stop at home real quick to change and then I'll pick you up."

"Sounds good." I take a deep breath and look at the spot where I'd seen the man. Logan could take me to ride every roller coaster in the US and I'd happily leave this room to go with him. "I'll wait downstairs." After I hung up, I was on my feet. I moved in a flurry, shaking the whole time. I needed to get out, get away from whatever living nightmare I seemed to be dealing with. I didn't even look in the mirror once I was dressed, I just slipped on my shoes and grabbed my overnight bag Ava helped me pack earlier. I was going to smile and make it through this dinner, then I was going to spend the night with my boyfriend, and I was going to be normal. I would not become my mother. I would not let this get to me.

"Autumn, it's so nice to meet you!" A friendly woman greeted me with a huge grin the second Logan led me through the door. I was still a little shaky, but I got through the drive to his parent's house. His mother, Angela, hugged me, and the smell of cinnamon and fresh bread clung to her. This is how a mother is supposed to smell. Not like alcohol and sweat. "Your father will be home in a minute, you know he's always running late." She spoke to Logan once she let me go. He simply nodded and led me into the living room where his older brother sat with a laptop.

"Hey there, little bro." His eyes flashed to me and he sent a conspiratorial wink. "How much did you pay her to act as your girlfriend? She's too pretty for you."

Usually someone talking about my looks would make me uncomfortable, but he was clearly teasing Logan and his smile drew me in. The entire house gave a sense of safety and warmth. Is this really how other homes felt? Was my life truly this lacking?

Logan made the introductions. His brother, Thomas, worked as a mechanic. They looked similar with blue eyes and dark brown hair, but his was nearly shaved off, and his arms and chest were wider. Glancing between them, I got the feeling Logan took after his mother a little more in the shape of his eyes and mouth.

"I'm so glad you could join us, Autumn. Logan thought you had plans with your father and wouldn't be able to come this time. I hope you are okay with lasagna? I would have asked for your preferences but Logan didn't tell me it would work out until earlier and I already had this prepared. It's Tommy's favorite."

"No, lasagna sounds great! I can't say the last time I had that. Thanks for having me on such short notice. A nice homemade meal beats the granola bar and orange I had planned."

"Oh dear, we can't have that! I made cookies earlier, you make sure you take a bag home with you before you leave." I glanced at Logan, my eyes wide. Is she for real? He seemed to read my expression because he grinned and gave a small nod. The door opened and Angela held up a finger, "that must be Michael. Everyone can go ahead in the dining room."

Logan caught my hand as I followed Thomas. "So, now I think you have to introduce me to your dad."

"I guess so." It was a sobering thought. I looked around his home, pictures hung all over the walls, the doorway actually had the boy's heights measured out, the hardwood was nicked probably from one of them bouncing a ball in the house or something silly. I thought of the small house I'd grown up in. What would he think when he saw my life intimately? It was one thing for me to tell him, it was another to witness it, be a part of it.

His father came in as we were seated and my thoughts were confirmed. Thomas was almost an exact replica of his father. Michael's face was lined though, deep grooves on his forehead but also around his mouth like he smiled a lot.

"Logan, you actually brought her! I thought you were making her up."

"Funny, Dad."

"You know, I'm the older brother here and no one ever asks me to bring over a girl."

Michael rolled his eyes. "That's because you are gay, son. If you brought over a girl, there would be other questions involved. How is Will?"

"Yes, I was so disappointed he couldn't come with you on this trip."

The conversation turned to what Thomas and Will had been up to recently, and I forced the heavy dinner down. Every bite was delicious, but I felt my stomach fill and had to fight the internal struggle of wanting to clean my plate or running to the bathroom to empty my stomach. No one else seemed to have the same problem. The men were all going in for seconds and when Logan saw my frowning at the rest of the food on my plate, he secretly swapped it with his empty one. He was always looking out for me.

CHAPTER 8

That night, I went with Logan back to his place. The others were home, still up and playing video games. They hardly glanced in our direction when we came in. I noticed Alice sitting on the sofa with her laptop. She was grinning as Jerry yelled about Levi shooting him in their game. Our eyes met, and hers gave a small roll. I wanted to get to know her better. Logan and I had spent most of our time at the park up in the tower ride, waiting to be rescued. It hadn't exactly made for a wonderful bonding experience with everyone else.

When we got to Logan's room, he gave me a full-on grin that took my breath away. He had far too much power over me. One look and I was begging for more, like a puppy lapping up attention. "So, what did you think of the family?"

"They are great. They make me think you're adopted though..." He tossed a pillow at me, but I just stuck out my tongue in response. "Seriously though, I don't think I could like them any more."

"Good. When do I get to meet yours?"

"Well, it's just my dad..." My fingers picked at the hem of my shirt as I mentally compared the grand differences between our upbringings.

"Yes, Jack Crowe, the dark poetry writer."

"You know, I told him you said that, and I think he's now debating a career change. He's ready to throw out his entire business to make it as a writer."

"I'm telling ya, all in the name." He moved in closer, his hand reaching out to take mine in his warm grasp. "But you aren't changing the subject."

"Maybe we can meet him at a restaurant or something soon. He's not really a cook, so it'd probably be easier." Plus, it would get me out of having to show him where I grew up. I wasn't sure if he sensed some deeper meaning, but he finally shrugged and accepted my answer. "Sounds good." He released my hand and put distance between us again, moving towards his desk against the opposite wall. "Now, are you all caught up on your reading for class tomorrow because I gotta say, I'm not..."

"I'll lend you my notes, but I was thinking of some other activities for this evening..." Something came over me, making me bold. I ate up the distance in two long strides until I was sharing his air. His expression changed and seeing his gaze gave me the rest of the courage I needed. My arms snaked around him and I found his lips with mine. Desire and hunger filled me to the brim, and I gave it all to him, only to have him return it in every small touch.

Then our touches and kisses became greedy, and we fell into the abyss with no desire to find our way back out again. He gave in to me so quickly, tugging at my bottom lip as his hands worked their way under my shirt. He didn't tease as he had in the viewing tower. This time, he pulled it over my head and let his hands explore all the newly exposed skin. I sucked in a breath when his fingers trailed down my spine. The small noise I made seemed to set him aflame, and he pulled my hips so I was flush against him.

"Are you sure?" His voice was husky and his grip on my hips tight like he'd tear someone apart if they tried to pull me away.

"Very." My voice came out breathy. I was aching to feel him. I may not have done this before, but my body seemed to know exactly what it wanted, and right now, it only wanted Logan.

"Always wanting to check things off that list of yours." He kissed at a tender spot on my neck that sent a shock right down to my toes. "Spend the night with the hottest guy in class." Teeth scraped over my shoulder, then my bra disappeared somewhere on the floor. "Check." Then I was in the air as he lifted me to place me on the edge of the bed. Before I could make a sound of surprise, his mouth was on my breast and I was arching against him, begging not so silently for more. Then my pants and his shirt joined the graveyard of clothes on the ground, and his mouth was roaming down my stomach. His fingers moved over my panties, and if his mouth hadn't come up to cover mine, I might have made some other sounds.

There was no shyness. I wanted him, *needed* him, and he seemed to feel the same way about me. My hands moved down his chest and found his pants. No fair for him to have on more clothes than me. He helped me take care of that, and jeans and boxers fell to the floor. It was clear he was more than willing to be with me, but he moved back between my legs before I could explore the situation further. His teeth scraped against my hip as he nipped and kissed around the edging of my panties before he pulled them down and let his fingers find the soft spot that shattered me into a million pieces.

"Logan." His name was a sigh, a beg for more, but when his mouth joined his fingers, I knew he was planning on making my torture last for some time. Everything in me came alive as his tongue flicked over me, tasting and devouring. Something overcame me and I ground against him, needing it all. He added another finger inside just as I dove over the brink, and I could feel him as I pulsed with pleasure.

"God, you're beautiful." He slowly pulled away from me, but before I could protest at the loss of him, he was pulling on a condom and settling on top of me. "Are you ready?" He kissed my collarbone.

"Please, Logan." I lifted my body to press against him and felt the hardness there. I was aching for more. He flashed a grin before taking my lips into a deep dance of seduction, then he was slowly moving inside me. I stretched for him, discomfort filling me for a moment as he settled deep in me, our bodies as one. He moved slowly at first, to let me get used to the feeling of him, but we were both desperate for more, and the moment I showed that hunger, he gave me everything he could. I felt his need for me, his tenderness and love. He made love to me, and I hoped I was giving just as much back to him as I moved to meet him, wrapping my legs around his hips to keep him close.

When we both made that last leap over the edge, he pulled me against him and pressed kisses to my shoulder. He pulled the blanket up over us and whispered words to me, but I was too spent to make them out. I drifted off, surrounded by him, my body perfectly heavy.

Class the next morning seemed to drag on. Logan broke the unwritten rules of changing seats mid-semester and sat directly behind me. Through the class he traced pictures on my back like he had last night as we drifted off to sleep. I couldn't help but smile at the thought. He had been tender and patient, and brought me to life. All I wanted to do now was curl up at his side and rest my head against his chest. Instead, I listened to the intense dissection of Piaget's Theory and tried to take notes. Afterwards, we grabbed lunch and headed back to his place. The idea had been to study and eat lunch, but quickly derailed into something much more active, and before I knew it, I had to head to my shift at the library.

The job was straightforward, and I liked the quiet. My primary job was to pull books on hold and put back the returned books. It kept me moving and awake, and gave me a chance to let my mind drift while my hands did busy work. My mind drifted to Logan and stayed there, refusing to look away from the beauty that had entered my life. I would do my best to resist pushing him away. If he wanted to meet my dad, I would make it happen. Meeting the parents simply meant we were moving forward.

Night was settling in, darkening the windows, lighting the books with fluorescence. We were coming up on closing time, which meant I'd be able to blast music over the speakers for the last hour while I finished up. I turned down a line of shelves with my book carriage, but hit something on the carpet, stopping the cart suddenly and sending a pile of books flopping to the floor.

It jabbed me in the stomach as I ran into it, and for a second, I lost my breath in a painful gush of air. It took a moment and a few deep breaths to get the sharp pain to subside. When it did, I moved around the cart to gather up the fallen heroes. Something grabbed my arm and the familiar dark figure appeared before me. I gave a squeak of fear and tried to tug free, but he had an iron grip on my arm, bruising me when I struggled.

"Autumn, you are mine. The longer you fight it, the more people I'll hurt. I'll take everything away from you until you come crawling towards me. Your mother named you after the season where everything dies. Your birth would kill her happiness. She never had any love for you. She wanted you dead the instant she found out about you, but I protected you in the womb. I protected you when she tried to take pills to get rid of you."

My breath caught. Had she really done that? Did she really try to get rid of me right from the beginning?

"This is real, isn't it? What are you? What do you want with me?"

He ran a finger over my jaw in a way that reminded me of Logan, but without any of the tenderness. A chill ran through me and I cringed as far away as I could.

"Leah sold the soul of her firstborn in order to capture the heart of the one she loved."

"Wha-what?"

"Jack never paid Leah any mind. He ignored her, had all these dreams about moving away, going to school to become an architect...Leah got desperate. If he left, she would never gain his heart...I didn't want to sit by and let that happen. She'd be heartbroken." He leaned back on his heels and released my arm. "So of course I swept in to rescue her. I can never overlook a damsel in distress. My first deal was for ten years of happiness, ten years, and then I would have her soul. But she wavered, so I gave another option. She could have a lifetime of happiness with Jack, I would just take her firstborn." He chuckled, and I felt sick. How many times had my mother said she needed to save my soul? I wanted to call him a liar, but it connected so many dots in my mind. While I cringed away from his words, a small voice in the back of my mind was accepting what he was saying.

"She thought she couldn't have children. She thought she would get everything she wanted without having to pay up. Leah was wrong. Now her payment falls to you. But I get the feeling you aren't just going to give in to me without a fight, so I'm going to show you a little of what I can do first."

Then, for the first time, he tilted back his hat so I could see his face. Dark empty sockets leered at me from a face covered in third-degree burns. His mouth was sewn shut and his nose was missing, just leaving two holes where it should be. A glass-shattering scream rang in my ears. The burn of my throat told me the sound came from me.

A student came running around the shelves, but the man was gone. "What is it? Are you hurt?" The guy crouched next to me and looked around, his face as white as a sheet. I couldn't answer, though. I looked down at my wrist and found finger-shaped bruises from where he had gripped my arm.

I barely made it through the rest of my shift. I couldn't explain to anyone what happened to me, so I just told them I startled myself when the cart got stuck. The guy that found me frowned at the story. He had found me on the other side of the cart crouched on the ground after all, but he didn't contradict me and the librarian on duty just covered her heart in relief.

Queasiness rocked me, my stomach doing somersaults as I tried to understand what was happening. Could my mother really have traded my soul for her own happiness? How could she even have that kind of power? While I wasn't a religious type, I was aware of the argument of humans being born with free will, which would put me in control of my soul. But maybe not, maybe since my whole birth happened because of the deal...I shook my head and started to leave after locking up. I was losing my damn mind, forget about my soul.

"Hey, good lookin'." I nearly jumped out of my skin at the deep voice, but Logan came running forward. "I'm sorry! Didn't mean to scare you. Sorry..." He chuckled at me, but I couldn't bring myself to smile. Everything was still too fresh. What was I going to do? Who do I even go see to discuss keeping my soul from a demon? "Hey, are you okay?"

"Yeah, just tired. Long day."

"Let me drive you back to your dorm." He took my hand, but then pulled it closer to his face. In the darkness, it was hard to make out, but he seemed to notice the bruising. I tried to tug out of his grasp before he said something, but we came under a light and he got a good view of clear finger marks. "What the hell happened?" He stopped dead in his tracks, his face suddenly red, his eyes ablaze. Normally, seeing him get so protective of me would make me feel good, but right now, I just wanted to get away.

"Nothing, my cart got stuck on something and I jammed it." I tried to tug away again, but he shook his head.

"Those are finger marks. You didn't have them earlier. Who did that to you?"

"Logan, please don't worry about it."

"You have to be kidding me..." He was pissed. He

stalked off, towing me behind. He parked his car on the street and he opened my door for me, but he didn't meet my eye. What could I tell him, though?

"Someone has been showing up...He was a...friend of my mother's. He showed up at the library today. This was an accident. He just grabbed my arm a little too hard. I bruise easily."

"Has he been stalking you?" He settled into his seat. This was as close to the truth as I could get.

"I guess...I've seen him a few times."

"Why didn't you say something? We have to tell someone. You can't just have some strange man showing up and following you all over the place!"

"I know, but it never seemed important before. Tonight was different though..." I thought of his threat and worried he would do something to Logan in order to teach me my lesson.

"Do you know his name? What does he look like? Did you tell your father? He might know him."

"Logan!" I wanted to reach up and cover my ears against his assault of questions. "I've had a long night. Can you just take me home? We can talk about it tomorrow."

"Maybe you should stay with me tonight." I could see

his worry, but I simply gave him a look. I didn't want him to be in the line of danger if something was about to happen. Plus, I needed some space to get a bit of research done. I needed to understand what was happening before I got anyone involved.

He read my expression and gave a sigh in response, but started driving toward my dorm all the same. He parked and jumped out, coming around to open my door, his gaze dark. "I'm going to at least walk you up and you are going to tell Ava about this guy so she can keep an eye out too." He held up his hand before I could argue. "That's all I request for tonight. We can figure out anything else tomorrow." It was a reasonable request after what I told him, so I agreed and leaned into him as we walked up to my dorm.

"No boys in your room this late at night, Autumn!" My RA saw us come up the stairs and gave me a firm look. She always looked away during the day but rules were rules, and she couldn't look away from a sleepover.

"I'm just walking her to her room. Promise." She nodded and disappeared. I peeked in my room first, just to make sure Ava wasn't walking around naked, but it looked like she wasn't in, so I let him follow me.

He immediately went into search mode, and went to

my closet to make sure no man was hiding there. I didn't look in that direction. The earlier vision of the man in the hat coming from inside the closet was enough to make me feel dizzy. I didn't want to be here, especially not alone, but more than that, I didn't want anyone to be in danger. The blinds near Ava's bed were still open, so I moved to close them when I caught sight of a foot sticking out from the space between the bed and the window. I froze for a split second while my mind raced to make sense of what I was seeing, but then I rushed forward.

"Ava!" She was sprawled out in the tight space as if she collapsed on the way to her bed. There was a thin foam around her mouth and she didn't have any color to her. I was on my knees beside her before Logan reached us. I felt for a pulse but there was nothing, no breath, no pulse....No Ava. I looked up and standing on the other side of the bed was the man in the black hat, though this time he hadn't bothered pulling the hat down. He smiled, his sharp white teeth glinting, and he shook a bottle of pills. I screamed. He disappeared, and it seemed Logan hadn't even seen him.

"Autumn, move so I can get to her!" He tugged me out of the way and crouched beside her, turning her on her side, trying to clear her mouth. He had started CPR when the

RA came running in, a bat in hand.

"Call 911!" Logan yelled while he did chest compressions. Somehow, the frenzy seemed to slow around me. I watched Logan going through the steps of CPR without pause. I watched the RA, Katie, talk to the operator of 911, but I sat frozen near the window. Suddenly fascinated with the curve of Ava's arch, I stared at the bottom of her feet. They swayed back and forth as Logan worked on her, jolted by the pressure he was putting on her body. But nothing changed. I went numb.

CHAPTER 9

"Give her some space!" Logan stood guard as the police tried to talk to me. The blinds were lighting up from the red and blue glow of police lights on the road. I sat on the edge of my bed and watched the flashing dance across the walls like I was at some kind of party. Somewhere in the back of my mind, I registered everyone in the dorm trying to peek in through the doorway, but I didn't care. I should care. I *should* cringe away from the attention, I should try to protect Ava, but I felt nothing.

"We really are sorry, but we need to ask her a few questions."

"I was with her. Ask me." I felt his hand squeeze my

shoulder, but it was almost like he was squeezing through a padded jacket. He answered the questions, but I didn't even hear them. What was the last thing I said to her? What was our last conversation? All I could see was the curve of her foot, bouncing back and forth. She was covered with a blanket now. A white sheet. She would have hated it. Her blankets were colorful, printed with huge flowers in bright colors. They should have put that over her. And she had been wearing her pajamas. Gray sweatpants and a long T-shirt she stole from an ex-boyfriend. She told me once she hated the band, but he loved it, and after she found him cheating on her, she told him she had lost it. It was a reminder not to settle. She had settled for him and got burned. If she was going to go into a relationship, she wanted something amazing. She wanted someone to take her breath away. She should have been in one of her bright dresses or her favorite jeans and one of her snarky t-shirts...

Suddenly, our last conversation crossed my mind and bubbles of laughter rose and escaped my throat. The police officer gave me a strange look, but I couldn't stop it, and soon I was holding my face to try to hide my giggles.

"Babe?" Logan's fingers brushed through my hair.

"I told her not to be a slut."

"What?" He sounded startled.

"Ava was going to meet some woman from her dating app, and was joking about how long it had been since," I glanced at the officer, who was observing me under bushy eyebrows, "since she had slept with someone. She quipped that if her date did at least half of the things right on their date, she was getting some, and I told her not to be such a slut. She stuck her tongue out at me and walked out. That was the last thing I said to her..." The laughter died on my lips. The last thing. She was my best friend and now she was gone. She had been my lesson.

The officer asked more questions about the guy she was dating, if she seemed depressed or stressed out. But I was the one who was always screwed up. She was happy. She was Tigger, and I was Eeyore.

"She was doing well in her classes...She was dating, but nothing serious. Ava was always happy."

"Well, it looks like she overdosed on some pills. We'll have to look into it more to find out exactly what she took. No one saw any notes or anything like that? A letter she left behind?"

"She didn't kill herself!" The man in the hat tricked her. He switched out her pills so instead of taking Advil, she took something else. Or maybe he just looked at her and she died. I didn't know how it worked, but he warned me I needed a lesson and this was it. He took away my best friend.

"Do you have somewhere you can stay? You shouldn't be here tonight. Especially not by yourself." He ignored my comment and his caterpillar eyebrows turned down in sympathy.

"Yeah, I live off campus. She can come with me." I didn't move, so Logan grabbed a bag and packed up some of my clothes, books, laptop, and my toiletry bag. He moved with authority, packing my things with precision, without doubt or question. When he thought I had everything I might need, he nodded toward the officer and took my hand.

I followed in silence and let him carry my bags. It wasn't until I was in his car that I came back to myself enough to realize the danger we were both in.

"Logan, she didn't kill herself." We sat in silence for what seemed like hours. Then he reached across and took my hand and started driving to his place. When we went in, Jerry, Alice, Riley, and Levi were all sitting downstairs watching a movie. Alice and Riley seemed to be working on something for one of their classes, while the boys played cards. They all looked up to greet us, but Logan shook his head, his body still radiating authority, and they all seemed to freeze in place. He took my stuff into his room and dug through a bag before tossing me something to sleep in.

"You change. I'll be back up in a minute, okay?" Logan kissed my forehead and left me standing there. He was telling them. He was telling them Ava died...*Ava died*. Ice ran through my veins as the thought settled in the pit of my stomach. She was dead.

"Why? Why did you do that? Why!" I searched the room but the man in the hat didn't show up. I tossed my clothes across the room and shoved on the pajamas, ripping at my hair when I tugged the shirt over my head. "Why?" And I wasn't numb anymore. A dam burst inside me and Logan returned to find me sitting on the floor with tears streaming down my face, my fingers pinching at the tops of my thighs as I fell apart.

Logan had his arm draped over me, pressing me against his chest. Every time he breathed it tickled my ear, but I didn't move. I don't know when I fell asleep last night. At some point, the tears just stopped, and I'd drifted off from pure exhaustion. Slipping out from under his arm, I stood and started toward the bathroom.

"Autumn." I spun at the female voice and faced my mother. Blood matted her hair, her skin was blotchy, and she stared at me through dead eyes. I wanted to scream, to run and hide, to give up and die already, but I just stared back.

"What did you do to me?" Maybe I really *did* go crazy somewhere along the lines, or maybe my dead mother really stood before me. She reached out her hand to grasp mine and when our palms touched, my body jerked and I was tumbling.

When I landed, I stood in an unfamiliar room. I was in a small trailer, and I was holding the hand of a teenage version of my mother. She was staring at a picture of my father in the yearbook, a red heart drawn around his face.

"Leah!" She jumped beside me at the harsh voice, and a man entered her room. In a second, she had the book closed and pushed away from her. It was then that I saw the bruises on her arms. "We have company. You be nice this time or there will be hell to pay. Do you understand me?"

She nodded, her whole body shaking in fear. The man, my grandfather, left the room and returned with a camera and a heavy older man with a comb over. The man leered at her, and all too soon, I understood.

"Stop it!" I turned away before the scene could unfold,

and then I was falling again. This time when I landed, she stood watching Jack laugh with his friends. She looked so frail and small, but she took a deep breath and walked toward him. She plastered a smile on her face and I watched as Jack, my father, turned, and after only a small glance toward her, walked right by. He was talking to his friends about the college he was accepted to, and I watched Leah's face crumble.

"Leah, I could help you." We both turned at the voice, and there stood the man in the black hat. He had it tilted to cover his face, but I knew what was under it. "I could get him to notice you. He'd save you from your father and his friends. Jack would save you from the camera. He'd love you. I could make that happen for you."

"How could you do that?" He smiled, and I got a glimpse of his sharp teeth once more before I was tumbling again. This time, my mother's arms held me as her hair whipped around my face. I was free falling, the ground was rushing toward me.

"I have to save your soul!" Her voice was shrill in my ear and then the ground found us-

"Autumn!"

I woke as my legs gave out from under me, and this

time, I was truly falling. Logan caught me with a small grunt, his eyes wide as he searched my face. "What the hell? What was that?"

"What?" I was groggy after the line of nightmares.

"You were standing on the damn dresser! How the hell did you even climb up there?" I tried to comprehend what he was telling me and looked at the dresser in wonder. "I was standing on that?"

"About gave me a heart attack. Damn woman, come on." He dragged me away from the spot as if he was too freaked out to stand there.

"I have to call my dad." I pulled away from him and grabbed my phone, which was still tucked inside my jean pockets. Logan called for me, but I was already out of his room and down the stairs. Everyone must still have been in bed, or off to their classes already, but I stepped outside anyway. The rush of cold air woke me up more. I was waking up to a world without Ava...

"Honey? What is it?"

"Dad, I need to talk to you."

"I guess it's a good thing you have me on the phone, then." He groaned. Clearly, I woke him up with my call.

"No Dad. In person, now. It's important."

"Autumn, what's going on?"

"When can you be here?" He seemed to catch on to my urgency, because we had a time and place to meet planned out before Logan came padding down the stairs after me.

"What's going on, Autumn?"

"We are going to meet my dad. Something very serious is going on and we need to talk about it."

An hour later, he drove me to the park near my father's current project so my dad could meet us. Logan was tense beside me. Not only was he meeting my father for the first time, but he also had no idea what we were doing. I wasn't sure *I* even knew.

"Dad!" I spotted him at a picnic table that stood away from the playground area, giving us privacy. He stood, the gray that was overwhelming his head of hair glinted in the sun as he came out from under the shade of a tree. His face was creased with worry and question, but he pulled me into a tight hug before turning his attention to Logan.

"Dad, this is my boyfriend Logan, Logan, this is my dad, Jack."

"Nice to meet you." My dad released me to hold out a hand to Logan, and they shared a firm handshake. "I'd tell you I've heard a lot about you, but that would probably embarrass Autumn." He flashed me a wink, and Logan grinned, seeming more at ease. "So I hate to ask, but are you two pregnant or something?"

"What? No!"

"Okay then, what is this about?" We made our way back to the picnic table, and I tried to think about how to start this conversation.

"Was Mom's father abusive?"

Dad and Logan both looked startled, but there was a resignation in my father's eyes. "Where is this coming from?"

"Because I think her father and his friends abused her and took videos. You guys believed that you couldn't have children, but then found out about me. You were going to go to college and become an architect, but I'm guessing out of the blue you noticed my mom and fell in love at first sight. So instead of going away to college, you stayed here and married her, and threw all the plans away that you thought you had."

His skin looked ashen as he stared at me. He'd never told me any of that, but the dream showed me, and somehow I knew it all had to be true. And if it was true, then the rest of it must be, too. "Dad."

"Who told you all that?"

"Is it true?" Logan reached over and gripped my hand as my voice rose.

"Yes." My dad croaked, still staring at me in wonder. "Who told you?"

This is where it would get tricky. I needed help to figure out what was happening to me and how to stop it, but how was I supposed to tell them without simply sounding crazy?

A cool hand rested on my right shoulder and I turned to see who was there, but there was nothing, and the feeling of a hand was abruptly gone. But it made me braver. "Mom told me. Last night, she showed me pieces of her past." Logan stared at me from the corner of his eyes, his eyebrows pulled down.

"What are you talking about?" My dad ran a large hand over his face, keeping his hand over his mouth as he looked at me.

"Mom wasn't crazy. There was a demon after her, and now it's after me. And he killed my roommate, Ava."

CHAPTER 10

My father's face steadily turned redder as he stared at me from across the table. Logan's hold on my hand loosened before he slowly withdrew from me. "You have to be fucking kidding me! Is this some college joke? Why would you think that anything about what you just said would be funny?" Dad's voice rose steadily as he talked to me, but I just stared at him.

It was completely out of character to see this kind of reaction directed toward me, but it brought back memories of him and my mother arguing.

"Dad! How else would I have known all that stuff? I kept seeing this man in a black suit and hat. His skin was burned away, he didn't have eyes, and he had teeth that were sharp like daggers. I just keep seeing him!" I turned to Logan now, though he didn't meet my eyes. "When I got really sick? I saw him for the first time. I saw him and my mother in the hallway, and I was so afraid that I left my bike behind and ran back to the dorm. Then I just went into some trance and got sick. I thought it was just stress at first or something, but I kept seeing him. He told me mom sold my soul-"

"Stop this right now! I spent years listening to Leah go on and on about demons and angels and all that bull. I watched her fall apart before my eyes, going on and on about how she made some deal with a demon. She was an alcoholic! She was unwell!"

"What if she wasn't, though? Dad, he told me she exchanged my soul in order to get you to fall in love with her-"

"Stop! I loved her. Some *demon* didn't make me do anything."

"Please, just listen to me!" Logan reached out and put his hand on the small of my back, but I pulled away. "Dad, she didn't think she could have me. She thought she could get you to love her, and then she would never have children, so she would never have to pay him back. Was she ever happy about me? Did she ever get excited about the idea of having a child?" He stared at the table, but he at least wasn't yelling at me. "She changed after me, didn't she? She changed, because she knew I wouldn't bring happiness...not really. Because *he* was going to come for me." I reached across and held his hand. "Dad, he's here and I don't know what to do. I need help."

"Autumn, we can get you help." He squeezed my hand, and I felt hope. "I can set up an appointment with a psychiatrist...maybe we could get you on some medication to help."

"Dad..." He blurred as tears filled my eyes. "Dad, you have to believe me." He pulled his hand from me and stood, looking down at me over his nose.

"I love you, honey, but I can't help you with this. You need a professional to talk to."

"No! I'm not crazy!" I shot to my feet and slammed my palms on the table. I needed help. I *needed* him to understand. Maybe if he could tell me things mom said, or weird ways she acted it would give me clues.

"I'm not going down this rabbit hole again. You call me when you are ready to get help." And just like that, my father turned his back on me for the first time. I stared in silence as he retreated to the parking lot, and then disappeared from view.

"Autumn...maybe you *should* talk to someone. You've been through a lot. We all have nightmares, and stress can get to the best of us. Let's just go back and relax for the day, okay?"

"Logan! You saw me standing on top of a dresser! How did I know all of that about my parents?"

"You probably overheard things when you were younger and didn't realize, and now they are coming back to you." His voice was gentle, his gaze weary as he tried to reason with me.

"Sure, because everyone talks to their small child about that time their father and his friends raped you and recorded it, right?"

"I don't know. I also don't know any mothers that would jump off a bridge with their kid!" Regret flashed over his features as he realized what he said. "Autumn-"

"No, you're right. I'm all kinds of messed up. But that doesn't make me wrong. You knew Ava. Do you really believe she would kill herself?"

He sighed and rubbed a hand through his hair. He looked exhausted. "I don't know. You can't always know what someone is dealing with."

"Logan, my life could be in danger right now. I have to figure out what is happening and how to stop it."

"I really think you should talk to someone...your best friend just died."

"No." I managed to put strength behind the word. As insane as it all sounded, I knew I was right, and being put on medications would not help me fight back.

"Autumn, I think you need to figure some stuff out, and I don't know how to help you." He ran a hand through his hair and let out a deep sigh.

It hurt more than I was expecting. A void opened up in my chest, but I couldn't fight this, not when I knew I was right. "Right...I get it. It was fun while it lasted and all that."

"Autumn...I care about you. I'm not the kind of person to just sit aside when someone is suffering. I can't make you accept help, though, and I can't just watch this, and not help you. You think you are seeing *a demon*...You just have a lot going on, and you need a way for your mind to work through that. I understand that, but you need to talk to someone who can help you sort through-"

I needed to get away. This backfired in the worst way. I needed people, and my best friend just died, and the two men in my life turned their backs on me because they thought I was crazy. "I know how it sounds, I do." I chewed on my lip and pinched the top of my leg while I tried to concentrate on this conversation. "I'm not making this up. Something is happening, and I am scared. My lip trembled, and when Logan noticed, he stepped forward and pulled me into the warmth of his embrace.

"You've had to deal with so much terrible stuff in your life, Autumn. I know that. I can't understand how hard all of this has been for you, and I won't pretend to. You should talk to someone who can help you. You said you went to therapy before-"

"I don't need therapy right now, I need..." Hell if I knew what I needed. Probably a freaking exorcism. "What I *need* is someone to believe me, and if you can't, then you shouldn't be around me, anyway." With strength I didn't know I had, I escaped his grasp and started to walk away.

I had to walk away while I still could. I couldn't think of all that I was losing, or I'd stop fighting just to keep what I had. There was a bus that stopped at the park and drove through campus. I could catch that rather than sit in awkward silence with Logan. He ran after me, calling my name. I turned and met his deep blue gaze. All the humor that was usually in his features was gone, the warmth that he usually looked at me with was missing and replaced with worry.

"It's over, Logan. I need some space right now." I know he stayed and watched me for a little while, but finally the bus pulled up and I climbed in without a backwards glance. Maybe this was better. If this demon could kill Ava, then it could kill Dad, or Logan, too. So it would be better to be alone, fewer people in harm's way because of me that way.

I walked back to my dorm, and tried to come to terms with the fact that Ava had been alive yesterday morning...Yesterday, I thought I was just hallucinating while stressed. I thought I was my own person. Now I'd learned the truth, and it was time to figure out how to beat this. The floor was deserted, so I snuck back into my dorm and stood in the doorway for a few minutes. Ava had died in this room. It was my fault.

"Just give in, Autumn." There he was, standing in the spot where Ava's body had been found. He tilted his hat back once more, giving me a full view of the black holes where his eyes should be. A chill ran down my spine, but I stood steady, tightening my hands into fists at my side. "Just give in and no one else gets hurt. Your suffering will be over. You know the truth now. You were born for me." His mouth twisted into a smile made for nightmares.

"Why don't you just kill me? Why do you have to keep playing these games?"

He moved in the blink of an eye and suddenly appeared right in front of me. He reached out and grabbed my throat, pinning me to the wall with unimaginable strength. "Is that what you want? You want me to kill you?" I struggled to breathe, but he cut off my airways completely. Adrenaline pumped through me, but there was nothing I could do. With a sharp twist of his wrist, or another minute of just holding tight, I could be dead.

I thought of the years where I'd slowly been killing my body. Those years where I'd danced right on the line between life and death, as I dealt with my depression and self harm, while still wanting to live. I wanted to live. I'd fought to bring myself from that dangerous line, and I'd fight now. My will to live was so much stronger now, and I would not give in to this demon just because of something my mother had done. I clawed at his gloved hand, but couldn't find a purchase. I kicked my feet, which were now dangling above the ground. He just leered at me, his teeth gleaming.

"You are mine. All you have to do is say it." He released me without warning, and I crumpled to the floor with a soft thud.

"No." My voice was raspy and the single syllable hurt me to speak. I glared back at him, staring into the pits of his eyes.

"Wrong choice, Autumn. Now the real fun begins." And he was gone once more, leaving me to wheeze in each breath on the floor of my dorm.

The rest of the week, I didn't go to class. A counselor came to see me. She was upset that I went back to my dorm, but I insisted on staying, so she finally left it alone. She also sent pardons to my teachers, which allowed me the week off to mourn, but I knew they would expect me back the following week. They invited me to speak with the counselor whenever I needed, but I knew I wouldn't go.

After a week of hardly any sleep, I felt ragged. I kept seeing the demon everywhere. I had long scratch marks on my upper thighs and no recollection of what happened, other than waking up to my legs hurting. Logan texted to ask how I was doing and if he could come and check on me. When I didn't respond, Alice joined Riley on her visits.

The dorm building had a small memorial for Ava. She had been popular and made friends with everyone she came in contact with. They lit candles for her and left notes, flowers, and balloons at the tree across from our room. I didn't go, but I watched from the window. It was beautiful. She would have liked it.

It had now been two months since my birthday, and everything had changed. I needed to stop what was happening to me. The internet provided information about demons, but everything I saw regarding possession left me feeling lost, and more out of control.

Finally, I forced myself to prepare for psych class, having zero desire to run into Logan or face any of the other students. It seemed everyone knew I was Ava's roommate and that I returned to our room. When I left for food or research, I felt every eye on me, and heard the whispers that followed me.

I missed my bike as I walked across the campus to my lecture building. Logan was already inside, still in the seat behind my empty chair. I had timed it so I would get there just before class started. I felt as everyone turned to stare at me when I walked into the room. The professor gave me a sad smile before getting to work, pulling up her notes for the lecture.

Logan met my eyes and frowned as he searched my

face. I wondered what he saw there. I hadn't bothered to look in the mirror after my shower this morning. Every time I looked in the mirror, I felt like I was staring at a stranger. Instead, I had tied my hair back and avoided the mirror Ava had hung at the door.

It didn't seem Logan liked what he saw in my face. I couldn't blame him. Sleep had escaped me and three times I woke up in an odd spot in the room. The most discerning was when I woke up in the same spot Ava died. Large, dark circles had appeared under my eyes, and just kept getting darker. Food tasted like ash on my tongue, and it became far too easy for me to skip meals a day at a time. I now lived in a constant state of nausea, but food, or the absence of it, didn't seem to make a difference.

"Autumn..." His voice sounded odd and broken as he drew out my name.

I spotted an empty seat in the back of the room, so I took it before he had the chance to say anything more. The lecture started, but Logan stared at me, half turned in his seat, ignoring the people that sat between us. Careful to avoid eye contact, I pulled out my laptop but didn't bother pulling up my notes for class. Instead, I pulled up the best website I found about deals with demons, and spent the period reading it over. By the end, however, I felt only one choice remained. I would have to find a priest.

A quick search came up with an older church just off of campus. Jotting down the address, I closed my laptop just as the lecture ended and pulled out the work the professor had sent over for me to keep up. Logan was waiting for me at the door, a silent statue watching me, but I turned my back to him and went to the desk.

"Thank you for the notes and everything. It was very helpful."

"Glad to see you back, Miss Crowe. If you have questions, or need any help, please let me know. I'll be happy to extend office hours if you need some extra help."

"Thank you, but I think I'll be okay." It felt odd to carry out an entire conversation after so much time on my own. Ava had always been chatty and got me to open up. Now, I don't have anyone.

"You look awful. Where have you been all week?" Logan still waited at the door and dove right in as I walked by him.

"My dorm." I held my bag closer and picked up speed. I didn't want him with me. I didn't want him telling me he couldn't believe me and then checking up on me. My answer seemed to give him pause, and he fell behind.

"Autumn..."

"Nothing has changed, Logan." I stopped and glared at him. "So leave me alone." Right behind him stood the man in the black hat. My eyes grew wide as I stared over Logan's shoulder.

"You have to take care of yourself. I don't want anything to happen to you." He touched my hand to hold it, but I jerked away, shaking my head.

"The only thing I have to do is stop what is happening, and being with me just puts you in danger." His gaze fell, but it gave me a chance to get away.

"You are mine, Autumn. You are already so alone in this world. Let me have you."

"Shut up!" A few people looked at me as I yelled out to my personal demon. He chuckled and pulled his hat down, but continued to follow me. It was a few blocks to the church and the entire time the man, no demon in the hat, hummed some tune while walking behind me. I wanted to rip out my hair and cover my ears, but I did my best to ignore the humming as I made my way to the church. Dead leaves crunched under my feet. Somehow I missed the beauty fall could bring. I hadn't even noticed the leaves changing color, and now they were dead on the ground. It felt ominous, and my heart grew heavy. Maybe there was nothing I could do. Maybe the demon would win and it would take my life away as a price for my parent's love.

The church came into view: gray-stoned, with classic stained-glass windows, and a large, heavily adorned wooden door arched at the center. It also had a small bell tower, but I knew it didn't chime anymore.

"No, Autumn...I can't let you go in there." The demon came to stand beside me. I still needed to cross the street in order to get to the church, but his words seemed to hold me in place.

A cool breeze whipped at my hair, taking me back to being on the ride with Logan. I was there again, sitting at the top with nothing to stop me from falling over, dropping to my death like my mother.

CHAPTER 11

"Excuse me, miss? Are you okay?"

I blinked, and a priest was standing before me. I darted a look to my right, but the demon was gone. There was something else that startled me, though. The street lights were on, the sky growing dark as I stood there. I felt frozen down to the bone, the joints of my fingers protesting when I tried to open and close my fist. The priest, a clean shaven older man, was staring at me with watery hazel eyes. "I belong to the church across the street. My name is Father Daniel. I noticed you standing out here an hour ago. I just saw you were standing in the same place. Are you okay?"

"An hour? What time is it?"

"Nearly five-thirty." I gasped and covered my mouth. I got out of my class at noon. How was that possible?

"I'm so cold..." Slowly I felt the ache and chill in my body.

"Come inside with me. We'll get you warmed up." He wrapped an arm over my shoulder and gave my arm a vigorous rub to get the blood flowing again. As soon as the light for the crosswalk said we could, he led me toward the church. My knees still seemed frozen, and it hurt to walk.

We got halfway across the street when the demon appeared on the sidewalk across from us. He simply shook his head at me and I faltered. I didn't have the chance to react further before the world erupted around us with the sound of squealing tires. I turned just in time to see a car going too fast coming at us. Father Daniel saw it too and pushed me forward, but he didn't move in time. A sickening thud sounded out as the car hit him, sending him flying until he landed on the street behind the car, which had finally stopped.

There was a scream coming from somewhere. It wasn't until I was on my knees beside the priest that I realized I was the one screaming. Chaos broke out as the driver got out and people from nearby ran over. Someone yelled to call 911, but

I just stared at the crumpled body in front of me. Father Daniel landed on his stomach, his one arm jutting out at an odd angle, his neck twisted in a way that told me he wasn't alive. I still checked for a pulse, but my fingers came back sticky with blood and no sign of life.

Someone in a black cloak ran past me and settled on the other side of what used to be Father Daniel. He had thick brown hair and a priest's collar. With one look, he seemed to come to the same conclusion I had. He made the sign of the cross and touched the older man's hand as he gave last rites. Sirens filled the air, and he finally looked up to meet my gaze.

"Are you okay?" He reached out to touch my arm, but I jerked away. There was no sign of my demon now, but I was sure he killed Father Daniel somehow. Who knew what he would do to this priest? "Are you hurt?" He insisted, even as he dropped his hand away from me. I shook my head. "He pushed me out of the way." Paramedics started running toward us and a police officer arrived and helped me to my feet.

Somehow, I found myself in the back of the police car while everything moved in a flurry outside the windows. The old man's kind face swam before me. It was my fault he was dead...just like Ava. I looked down at my palms and found them covered in blood. The police officer returned to find me sobbing. He wrapped an arm around me and sat beside me until I was done. It reminded me of Logan so much it hurt. "I just need your name and a number to reach you." His voice was soft, he was much nicer than the police officer that came to my dorm. "The driver gave a statement, but just in case we have other questions." He jotted down my information and handed me a tissue. "Where can I drop you?"

We rode in silence to my dorm building. I lost hours standing in front of the church. It had only felt like minutes to me. Realization that I only ate a granola bar today hit me, but I couldn't think of getting something to eat. I was already losing weight, and I knew it wasn't healthy, but what did it matter? I was already losing this fight, and I hadn't even started fighting yet. This demon took away my best friend and a priest I was seeking for help. He turned my father and boyfriend against me...I was alone. Utterly alone. I understood now how my mother could drink until she was delirious. She knew the truth. For the first time in years, I wished she was here. I wished more than anything I could sit holding her hand and tell her what was going on.

The officer asked if I would be okay and handed me

his card as I climbed out of the car, swinging my bag over my shoulder. I almost asked him to take me away and lock me up, but the demon would probably kill him too in some horrible accident and he was too nice for me to risk it.

When I got to my dorm, I fell to the floor by my bed and pulled my knees up to my chest. I needed to wash and change my clothes. I needed to get food. My homework was piling up, and I needed to work on it. The floor was hard on my bottom and my legs began to fall asleep, but I just concentrated on breathing.

"Autumn, I know you don't want all this pain. Think of how many more could die. All you have to do is give in to me and I'll make it all go away. Wouldn't that be nice?"

"Leave me alone. My mother is dead, don't you have her? Isn't that enough?"

"The deal was for you. Just think, your parents had twenty-odd years of happiness together. Your soul gave them that. What higher purpose could there be?"

"You killed that priest...he was just helping me, being a good person, and you killed him. Why? Ava was supposed to be some lesson of your power, but why the priest?"

"I told you I couldn't let you in that church." That's how I lost time...What did he do to me to make me stand frozen to my spot like that? "Poor Ava...she was excited about this new guy she was dating. She was waiting for you to get back so she could tell you all about it. Then she got a headache...she just kept taking pill after pill as if she forgot. She cleaned out the cabinet. Every pill the two of you owned between you. Then she got tired and went to lie down. You weren't here. If you had been here, you could have saved her. And that priest," the demon shook his head sadly, "wanted to help people since he was a little boy. He was one of the good guys, you know? Looked for people to help. He saw you. You looked like you needed help. And now he's dead."

"Fuck off." I looked up and met the darkness where his eyes should be.

"Ohhh, the little girl knows some bad words." He got in my face. I should feel his breath on me, smell him, but there was nothing. "Did your mother teach you that? Was it before or after she tried to kill you?"

He looked toward the door, and two seconds later, I heard a knock. The demon cocked his head at me, waiting for me to run for the door, but I continued to stare him down.

"Who could be coming to see you? You don't have anyone anymore. All you have is me." He held out his gloved hand, silently telling me to take it. I pulled my knees tighter to my chest and squeezed my hands together until they felt numb.

"I said fuck off."

"Autumn. I just want to make sure you're okay?" My door opened and Logan peeked his head in. The demon gave a sharp smile and ran for the window, leaping out even though it was closed. "Autumn? My dad called me to see if you were okay. He told me what happened." Logan's face lacked color and his eyes were wide with worry. For a second, I thought he might have seen the demon too, but he was looking at me, not staring out the window.

"I'm not the one that was hit by a car. I'm fine."

He closed the door with a heavy sigh and came to sit beside me. "I'm sorry."

"For what? Not believing me? Sorry I saw an innocent man die because I went to him for help? Sorry that you think I'm crazy? Just leave, Logan."

"No."

"Please. I can't do this right now." He flinched when my voice cracked.

"You need someone with you." He just didn't understand that there was always someone with me now. All I wanted to do was curl up at his side, but I couldn't do that.

"You are in danger by being here. Go home." I met his gaze, and he searched my face.

"What happened today?" It looked like he was going to reach for my hand, but when I made a fist, he let his hand fall to his side. "Tell me what really happened, Autumn. I promise I will listen."

Maybe I was just so desperate for someone to be on my side that I leaned a little closer until our shoulders touched. "I walked to the church to ask the priest for help. Stood across the road from it for hours. I had been there since class ended. I didn't realize the time was passing...He held me there. He told me I couldn't go to church."

I waited for Logan to argue that there was no "he," but he sat and waited for me to finish. "The priest saw me standing out there and came to offer me help. He was walking with me to cross the street and go inside when the demon appeared on the other side of the road...Then the car came. Father Daniel pushed me to safety the very last second-"

My words choked off, and I looked back down at my hands. Was that really his blood still there on my palms or was I just seeing it? "I could have died, but it wasn't me he was after. He told me he couldn't let me in the church, and he stopped me. It's over. I know you don't believe me. I know it sounds crazy. But no one is safe as long as I am around, especially you or my father." We sat in silence for a little while before he got up and walked out. So that was that. It was what I wanted, but genuine fear settled in at the thought of being by myself. What would happen when the demon finally took me? Would I become possessed? Simply die? Would I have to suffer in Hell for all eternity?

My door opened again, and Logan returned with a handful of wet napkins. "You should wash off your hands and change your clothes. Then you and I are going to see if we can find information on this demon of yours."

"What?" I took the napkins and scrubbed the blood on my palms, not sure if I should be relieved that it was real and not a hallucination.

"If you really believe this is what's happening, I'm all in. I'll help you." Yes, yes, please! I wanted to jump up and down. I wanted to cheer, but I shook my head instead. "Were you listening? Ava is dead and Father Daniels is dead. You can't help me. No one can."

"I believe that's my choice, not yours." He looked me over and I felt his assessment. "Have you been eating?" He watched me wring my hands together and shook his head.

"Start pulling up all your research so far. I'll order food." I opened my mouth to protest again, but he just held up a hand and was already going through his cell phone list. I was well aware he had multiple places on speed dial.

Little by little my hope came back to me. I watched as he placed an order for delivery, getting me a buffalo chicken salad and a hoagie for himself. I pulled out my small notebook of jumbled bullet points and opened my bookmarked pages. In all my searching, I hadn't found anything that looked like my demon, or anything that talked of someone trading someone else's soul.

We reviewed everything I had, and Logan took over while he forced me to eat. The salad he ordered for me was my favorite from the restaurant, but it was still surprising I could get it down. I wondered what it meant for us that he was here. Did he really believe me now? Did he want to get back together? What the hell was I doing thinking about boys when my very soul could hang in the balance?

"Every single thing I see about possession of a soul involves free will. Do any of these demons look familiar?" He pulled up a screen with sketch after sketch of demons. I scrolled through each one and ignored the fact my demon ran around wearing a hat like he lived in the 1940s and focused on the features of his face. The sharp white teeth, the burnt skin and burned away nose, the absence of eyes...Nothing quite fit what I saw, but I pointed out features that were in other sketches and Logan saved all the pictures I pointed out. I watched as he cut away the parts I mentioned and felt the warmth from him radiate into me. Right now, I need that warmth. It was as if the chill from earlier had settled deep within me and took hold. Nothing I did now could bring back the warmth I once knew.

Logan turned the screen back to me and I saw my demon. I almost asked him to pull a picture of a hat to place on his pieced together picture, but decided that might sound just a little too crazy.

"Tomorrow, I say we take this to the church and ask about it."

"No!"

"I'm not finding anything like this online. I think the first step to figuring this out is to find out what this demon is, or rather, who."

"Father Daniel died today because I tried to go into his church! If I stepped inside, it would probably blow up or something, killing all of us."

"Well then, I'll go on my own."

"You can't do that! I can't let anything happen to you." He sighed wearily and looked at the door to my dorm room. It had gotten late and the RA would not approve if she found out he was still in here, but I didn't really care. I didn't want him out of my sight, even if being away from me would make him safer. "We can figure something out in the morning. I should probably get out of here before you get in trouble."

"Please stay. I haven't been able to sleep...I may have a chance if you are with me." I waited for him to tell me we weren't back together, that he just wanted to help me. But he smiled and pulled back the covers of my bed and motioned for me to join him. I was exhausted. My body ached and my full stomach made me feel drowsy after going so long with the bare minimum. I didn't like how much I needed him right now, but when I settled down beside him and rested my head on his chest, I couldn't bring myself to care. For tonight, I would just pretend to be a normal college girl, spending the night with her boyfriend.

"Good night, Autumn. I'll be right here." He kissed the top of my head and played with my hair as the darkness pulled me into its embrace.

CHAPTER 12

The church loomed before me, beckoning me with warm light. The warmth seemed to envelop me in a hug, drawing me closer. I came to the street and saw where Father Daniel was struck by the car. There should've been blood on the ground, but there was no sign anything had happened other than a few small car pieces sitting at the edge of the road. They must have washed the blood away. Something about the idea of dragging out a power washer to wash the blood of a priest down the drain seemed dirty to me. It was early morning, and the road was deserted. It would still be another three or four hours before the sun decided to wake, but here I stood.

The light from the windows left a colorful reflection on the grass below; it seemed to make a statement. Though the priest was gone, the church would still leave its mark. It could not be erased. Which meant I could still get help from them.

I walked out into the street to cross, but the second I did, my feet seemed to be sucked into the earth, holding me still and giving me no chance to escape. Heart racing, I tried to scream, tried to beg for help. Out of the gutter was an awful gurgling noise and, when I looked, I saw blood rising from the depths, gushing out and filling the street. It reached me before I could take two breaths, and I struggled harder as the blood quickly reached my ankles, staining my skin with my crime.

"Please! Stop it!" I was sobbing now, covering my eyes from the sight of the deep red liquid washing over me. Nothing could block out the smell, though, the taste of copper filling the back of my throat. I was gagging and struggling to free my feet from the street. Nothing would let me move.

"Give in to me, Autumn. I can make it all go away." The whisper brushed against my ear and I tried to jerk away. Hands gripped my shoulders, holding me to the spot, as if I could've run away, with my feet planted as they were. "So much blood...All for you. Your mother, Father Daniel, poor Ava-"

"Please, stop. Let me go!" I jerked an elbow back and felt it connect with something solid. A breath rushed past my face as he let out a spurt of air at my attack. But then someone hauled me from the ground and threw me.

"Autumn!" A voice wheezed at me. It wasn't the demon's, but it *was* familiar. The grass was cool under my face and hands, and the smell of dirt helped wash away the sickening scent of blood. I took a deep breath to gain my bearings before I turned and found Logan standing at the edge of the road, bent over, his hands on his knees.

It suddenly occurred to me to wonder what I was doing out here, and why I was still in my pajamas, barefoot. "Logan? What are we doing here?" I realized belatedly that it was him I elbowed in the stomach, and he was struggling to gain his breath.

"You tell me. I woke up, and you were gone. I saw you running from the dorm window. You had a decent head start, but I caught up to you. I got here, and you were just standing in the middle of the road. You must have been sleepwalking."

Had I been sleepwalking, or did my demon bring me

here? "I'm sorry I hit you. I was dreaming the demon was standing behind me, telling me to give in. He was holding my shoulders and my feet were stuck in the earth. Are you okay?"

He gave me a wry grin and came to sit next to me in the grass. "I'm fine. I was just already out of breath from running all the way across campus after you, and then you knocked the air out of me. What else do you remember?"

"I just remember being here at the side of the road. I was staring at the church and where Father Daniel died. When I walked out into the road, I got stuck and blood started filling the streets-"

My voice choked off when I glanced down and saw blood stained my feet and the hem of my sweatpants. Logan followed my gaze, and his jaw dropped open. A second later, he was back on his feet and looking at the street. It was once again clear of blood and looked the same as it had when I got there. When he turned and met my gaze, there was no sign of his easy smile. He looked like he might pass out.

"It's all true, isn't it?" I watched as he came to terms with everything I'd been saying. "I mean...I wanted to help you, but I thought if I walked with you through this a little, then you would realize it wasn't real. That it was something else. Maybe one of your mother's abusers came back. You said someone was stalking you. I saw bruises on your wrist. Maybe they said something to you that triggered all this. But there is actual *blood* on your feet. You had a head start, but not so much so that you could have done something like this in your sleep..."

"Logan? Are you okay?" It was my turn to move to his side and give him support.

"How the hell is this possible? I mean, this stuff is just for the movies..."

"I understand how you feel. I'm still not sure I believe it, and I'm living it." Reaching over, I rubbed his back as he continued to stare in shock.

"That picture of the demon...you've actually been *seeing* that?" He turned and brushed my cheek with his hand. The tender touch was enough to calm me. "I'm so sorry, Autumn. I didn't believe you. I'm so sorry."

I grabbed his hand and held it against my cheek before he could pull away, then stood on tiptoes to kiss him. I needed the contact, and I thought he needed it, too. His hesitation ended quickly before he clutched at my hips and pulled me flush against him. All I wanted to do was get lost with him, forget all this death and pain, and enjoy what life had to offer. For so much of my life, I missed out on what was actually great, and now that I got a taste of it, my mother's choices were threatening to take it away from me.

"Take me home, Logan. I don't want to be here anymore." It came out in a plea, but I didn't care. He glanced at the church behind me and opened his mouth. I knew he wanted to argue that we should go there. We needed to sort this out. I knew, because I was thinking the same thing, but I kissed him again, and tried to clear both our minds. When I sucked on his bottom lip, he let out a hiss and started tugging me away. His place was closer, so we took off in that direction, though he moved carefully to keep me from stepping on anything in my bare feet. Everyone was still asleep when we got to the house, so he led me up the steps without fanfare and led me straight into the bathroom.

Without a word, he stripped us both down and turned on the water until steam rose. I didn't question and stepped inside while he lathered up his hands. His gaze turned hungry as he moved soapy hands over my skin. The hot water beat against my back and slowly loosened my muscles, relaxing me to a point of bliss. Logan crouched in front of me and slowly lifted one foot, washing away the dirt and blood before he did the same for the second. I felt a few cuts on the bottom of my heels from my apparent early morning run, but his hands soothed away the initial burn from getting soap in the cuts. More lather and he started moving his hands upwards, massaging my legs. It felt wonderful. Every ache and pain I had washed away with the water. The feel of his large hands moving over me had me moaning with a mixture of contentedness and burning desire.

"Logan." Goodness, I thought I'd lost all this, but now every stroke of his hand against my skin was sinful desire. He shushed me with a soft kiss and worked shampoo into my hair. I leaned my head back and closed my eyes, unable to fight the relief of my body. He worshiped me from head to foot - well, foot to head - and I would be lying if I said I wasn't enjoying it. As he washed away the shampoo, I took up the soap and lathered my hands, doing the same for him. His body was hard, with muscles from working out and training for the police academy. He was still two years away from his bachelor's degree before he would enter the academy, but I knew it was more of a lifestyle for him than anything else. He had his goal in mind, and everything he did was to work toward it; except for me.

His eyes closed as my hands washed him, his member hard when my fingers roamed over him. I gave a small smile at his reaction, but continued on to shampoo his hair and massage his scalp, as he had for me. He turned away from me for a moment to get his head under the water. I watched in silence as he washed away the soap and shampoo, and then we were drying off in a rush. Both of us felt the need to hurry, to be joined. My hair was still dripping when he laid me on his bed and demanded passion from my mouth. His hands continued roaming, worshiping, teasing, and pleasing. When I thought I couldn't take it anymore, he joined me and we rose together.

I woke some time later, my body disjointed and relaxed in a way I couldn't remember it ever being before. I stretched and my fingers touched a cool sheet as I reached Logan's side. My eyelids shot open. Panic settled down deep in my bones and I was up and dressed in record time.

"Logan?" I was shouting and didn't even know if his roommates were still asleep or not. I didn't care.

"In the kitchen!" He sounded calm, and very much alive, so I forced myself to settle down and found him smiling at me with pancakes cooking on the stovetop. "Are you okay?" He searched my face and his lips turned down a little.

"Yeah, yes. I just woke up, and you weren't there." I shrugged and kissed his cheek. He handed me a plate and quickly plopped three pancakes down before pointing to a small table they had in the corner. Syrup and butter were already waiting for me, along with a glass of orange juice. I raised an eyebrow in his direction.

"Breakfast is the most important meal of the day, and one of the few things I know how to cook is pancakes." I had to admit, they smelled heavenly. My stomach seemed ready for more food after he forced me to eat an actual meal yesterday, so I dug in as soon as he joined me with his own plate full.

"I think we have to go to the church today." I shot a look at him as he spoke. Since we came here in the early dawn, my life seemed normal again, better than normal, and now he wanted to bring it all back during breakfast. It ruined pancakes for me. "Autumn, clearly this demon is trying to keep you from the church. So obviously your answer has to lie there. If anyone can help you, it must be one of the priests."

"Mr. Hat already killed Father Daniel. A car could have hit me last night." Belatedly, I looked around to see if there were any signs of his roommates. I didn't exactly want them overhearing.

"Mr. Hat?" He asked dryly, a brow raised in confusion.

"He needed a name, and he never bothered to introduce himself." Logan shrugged at my answer, but I saw a smile playing at the corners of his lips. "Logan, I'm glad you believe me now, but you should walk away from me." I held up a hand before he could argue. "Clearly, Mr. Hat has the power to take us down if he wants to. I don't think he'll kill me though, because he wants me to give in to him. But you, anyone else I care about, he can destroy to get to me."

"I'm not leaving you to fight this alone." He rested a hand over mine. "Autumn, I love you. I'm not going anywhere." I should be more excited to hear him say those words, but it seemed loving me was only going to put him at greater risk, especially because I shared his feelings. "Stop, I see your mind working on how to get rid of me. It won't work. We are going to get ready and we are going to church." He took a bite before grinning again. "I should call my mother. She'll be happy to know I've decided to change my heathen ways."

CHAPTER 13

"Logan, are you sure you want to do this?" I helped him clean up from breakfast, and the ease of the morning quickly melted away. I kept seeing Ava lying lifeless next to the bed, her only crime being my friend.

"We have to figure this out. Once we get a better understanding of everything going on, then we will know how to fight back."

"Yes, but *I* need to figure this out. Not you. You have classes and work to worry about. You can't just drop everything and risk your life for me."

He turned toward me, his hair ruffled from running his fingers through. His eyes were dark with nervous energy, but his persistent smile tugged at his lips. "Autumn. I love you. You don't think *Mr. Hat* already knows that? He could use me against you at any moment, whether I'm at your side, or not. It's better we stay together and fight back." I sighed as he brushed back my hair and pulled me against him for a kiss. My dad's ringtone had us breaking apart. "Have you talked to him at all?"

"Not since..." I stared at his picture, taunting me from my phone. I had no idea what this conversation would be, or if I was ready. Logan gave my hand a squeeze and kissed my cheek. "I'll wait upstairs while you two talk."

"Autumn, where are you?"

"Hi Dad...I'm at Logan's. We were about to go out-"

"Well, I'm at your dorm building." Usually, that would make me happy, but his tone had me on edge. It wasn't often ·he talked to me out of anger. The tone I heard now was one usually reserved for my mother when she was caught doing things like driving drunk with me in the car.

"Okay...Is something the matter?"

"Just tell me how to get to Logan's. We'll talk about it then." My stomach flipping with worry, I gave him directions and hung up. I felt like a small child getting reprimanded.

"Everything okay?" Logan caught the look on my face

as he stood at the top of the staircase.

"I'm not sure. My dad is heading over..."

"Well, we can talk to him about everything going on. I'm sure together we can get him on board." I smiled at him. We sat on the sofa to wait for him to get there, but I felt unsettled. Something was wrong. Maybe he was just mad at me because of our conversation at the park. Maybe he was stressed out, and it just *sounded* like he was angry. Or maybe my demon had done something.

When he pulled up, Logan went to get the door. He barely got out a hello before Dad came storming in, his face red as he stared down at me. I've never been afraid of my father. It was always my mother that set me on edge, but there was something foreboding in his gaze that sent my heart racing. Logan seemed to feel it too, because he stood at the ready at my dad's side, as if he would jump him if needed.

"Mr. Crowe?"

"What the hell, Autumn? What the fuck were you thinking?" He was around the sofa in two long strides, and grabbed my arm, yanking me to my feet.

"Dad!"

"Is this some call for attention? You thought I would just come home and let it slide?"

"What are you talking about?" His fingers were bruising my arm, and I gave a small cry when he yanked me forward. Logan jumped into movement, putting himself between us and laying a hand on my dad's chest.

"What is this about?" His voice was stern and commanding, and I could see perfectly the police officer he would be. The fingers on my arm loosened as Logan twisted his body between me and Dad, forcing him to let me loose.

"This is between my daughter and me."

"Dad? What happened?"

"I've been away for work and I came home this morning to find my house trashed! Something you may have forgotten, because you went into the hospital not long after I had it done, but I had a security camera installed at the front and back of the house. So I went through it. Four days ago, you came home and ripped the house apart! And what's worse, you destroyed every one of your mother's pictures!"

Logan glanced at me. "It wasn't me! I would never do that. I forgot you were even going away, with everything that has been going on lately..."

"Right, your little *demon*. If you weren't my daughter, I would have you arrested. But since you are," I flinched at the way he spat the words, "I have another idea. We are going to get you some help whether you want it or not."

"Jack, I think we should talk about this. Autumn was telling the truth. She's in danger-" My dad flicked something into Logan's chest. He managed to catch it. I saw it was a picture of my parents together, but her body was covered in permanent marker, spelling out "whore" over and over.

"Dad, that wasn't me!" I wanted to be strong and commanding, but the way he was looking at me, and talking to me, sent me through the years to my mother talking down to me, hating me with her every breath.

"I have you on video, Autumn!"

"Wait! You were sleepwalking last night. You made it blocks, Autumn. Maybe you *did* go there and do this. You were just asleep. You weren't in control of yourself."

"That's almost ten miles away!" He shrugged, and I understood completely. With everything that has happened since my birthday, was I really surprised? The thought of me walking almost twenty miles to get there and back, destroying my father's possessions, and waking up in my dorm room really set me on edge. Who knew what else I had done this past week when I was completely on my own? The possibilities spread out before me and I thought I might be sick.

"Enough of this shit. You are coming with me, Autumn."

"What? No, Dad. This is real!" He pushed Logan aside and gripped my arm again, and started dragging me to the door. This was not him. Even angry, he wouldn't treat me like this. All my life, he had been nothing but gentle and caring towards me. "Dad, you are hurting me!"

"Jack, let her go!" Logan was back on his feet and running after us, but my dad swung around and pulled something from behind his back. A second later, he had a gun in his palm and had it pointed right at Logan's chest. Logan faltered to a stop and his eyes grew wide like saucers as he held up his hands. Everything went really still for a moment until I saw that my father's hand began to shake.

"Dad, stop it!" Logan shot me a worried look, but then we were on the move again, and Dad was shoving me into his car. He kept the gun pointed toward the house and I knew, without a doubt, this wasn't my father. This was Mr. Hat.

Logan came running out of the house as we pulled away, and he didn't pause. I watched from the window as he leapt into his car and pulled out to follow us. I wanted to tell him to just back off and stay safe, but my phone was still on the kitchen table, as was his.

"Where are you taking me?" I dared to send a look in my father's direction, but I no longer recognized the man sitting there.

"I'm going to get you help. You are very sick." He didn't look my way. His knuckles were white, and it looked like he was shaking, but I was too afraid to reach out and see. I knew he would feel wrong to me if I did touch him.

"Dad, I didn't do it. I swear. I'm not sick. There is something very serious going on here, and we need to get real help before it's too late."

"It's not worth trying, Autumn." Another voice joined us in the car, and I nearly jumped out of my skin as Mr. Hat appeared behind me. "He was under a very powerful blood pact. The love he has for your mother will never die. And you have been a very naughty girl. Going and destroying all her belongings like you did." I wanted to yell, but since it didn't seem my father could see him, I thought it would only prove that I was crazy.

"You never took Mom for help. She drank all the time, she talked to things that weren't there, she tried to *kill me*. Why didn't you send her to rehab? Why didn't you make her talk to someone? Dad, please."

"I tried, but she refused. But I will not sit aside again with you. I love you, and I know you have been through so much already. This isn't your fault. I'm sorry I got angry, but we are doing this. I won't sit aside and watch you fade away like your mother."

I wanted to argue, but I saw his pain. Maybe, if I was a stronger person, this wouldn't be happening. Maybe after years of hurting my body, punishing myself for the actions of my mother, some part of me had welcomed this. And it was killing my father.

We pulled up to a plain-looking building, and I followed him inside willingly. I didn't think my father was in complete control, and I would rather have to deal with whatever consequences than have *him* suffer for them. I shuddered to think where he even got the gun, as he had always been against them.

"Welcome to the Finch Street Wellness Center. How may I help you?" A pretty brunette with a soft smile greeted us. Cream tiled floors and calming green walls surrounded me. I almost turned to make a run for it. Out the front doors I saw Logan's car pull up, but I motioned for him to stop through the window. He paused and seemed to listen to me, because he stood just outside the door, but I had a feeling it was taking everything in him not to rush in.

"And will Miss Crowe be admitting herself?"

"No, I'm signing her in." I flashed a look at him, but he didn't look my way.

"I'm sorry, sir, but unless it has been court ordered, you cannot commit without an attorney of law." I watched as his fingers flexed toward the gun he had hidden.

"It's okay, I'd like to get treatment." The woman searched my face and I could see she was trying to gauge the situation. The last thing I wanted was to get committed to some mental health institute, but I also didn't want my father threatening anyone with a gun. I flashed a look back toward the doors and Logan took that as an invitation to join us.

"What exactly does that entail? What will happen if I sign myself in?"

"Autumn-" I shook my head before Logan could say something more.

"You will be taken off any drugs you are taking and we will walk you through your withdrawal period. You will be evaluated by a psychiatrist and a health plan will be made for you. We will observe you and you will attend both group and individual counseling sessions. Once the psychiatrist sees you, we will know the time of your stay better."

"I'm not taking drugs." She frowned at me and looked at my father again. "I have an eating disorder. I've been handling it well for quite some time, but the stress of college and classes," I motioned down to show the way my clothes were already hanging off of me. How many meals had I skipped? Also, they would see my medical background, so it wasn't a hard story to sell. Not to mention, I had been absent from my support group for a little over two months now.

"She also thinks a demon is after her." My father finally spoke up. Logan grabbed my wrist as the woman turned her attention away from me.

"What are you doing?" Logan hissed, trying to keep his voice down.

"What I have to do to protect the both of you. He's not in control, at least not completely..." I caught her eye, so I quieted and moved to grab Logan's hand for support. He squeezed and his thumb started tracing my palm. I wanted to stay with him. I wanted all of this to be over.

"Well, we will speak with your daughter and find out everything she is dealing with." She handed me a clipboard of papers to read over and sign.

"Dad, are you sure I have to do this?" I tried once more. He nearly growled in response, so I nodded and signed my own commitment forms. Wouldn't my mother be so proud?

CHAPTER 14

This wasn't how I expected my day to go. I was ushered deeper into the building, leaving behind my father and Logan with only a prayer they would be safe. The woman, Sherry, chatted away amiably, but her words were nothing more than a hum in the background. She showed me a room which I would have to myself for the time being, before taking me to be searched and given a "wellness center outfit" which consisted of light gray pants and a t-shirt with the name of the building on it.

Mindlessly, I went through the motions. I had to pee in a cup so they could test me for drugs. My belongings - the clothes on my back - were taken from me, and finally I was led into an office where I was told my counselor would come to meet me. Apparently, being twenty-one is awesome. *Really* been enjoying myself so far.

A woman joined me in a perfect librarian-type outfit including black rectangular glasses, a tight bun which made her light red hair nearly disappear, and a maroon pencil skirt with a matching jacket. I grinned stupidly as she settled down behind her desk and looked me over.

"Miss Crowe-"

"Please, just call me Autumn. If I'm going to divulge my secrets to you, we should at least be on a first name basis." I felt a little rude saying it, but she smiled at me before giving me a conceding nod. "Okay, Autumn, I'm Belle. You have decided to join us to work through a treatment program?" I shrugged in response. "It looks like you are clear of any drugs or alcohol. May I ask what brings you here?"

I decided to be as honest as possible with her. Bringing up a demon trying to take my soul would probably get me sent away to a far more serious institution, so I worked around that. "I have an eating disorder and it has become more difficult to deal with recently. My best friend...well, they believe she killed herself. This happened just over a week ago. She was my roommate. Then, two days ago, I was there when

Father Daniel was struck by the car. He was walking with me across the street." I knew both deaths had made the local news and papers. It was likely she knew about them.

"It sounds like you have been through a lot recently." You have no freaking idea, lady. I nodded and brought my arm around to hug myself. "Your father mentioned a demon when you came in?"

"I haven't been sleeping well." It wasn't a lie. "I've been sleepwalking, and I guess I've seen a few things just from lack of sleep." Belle nodded and took a few notes.

"I'm going to let you settle in today. Tomorrow we can meet together and talk more. Does that sound okay?"

"Sure."

"You are free to look around. There is a rec room of sorts just down the hall. Games, TV, crafts, books, just some things to make you feel at home. You may also retire to your room if you choose. Now, we follow a strict schedule and meal times. You will be allowed visitors during your stay here, but they are not permitted to bring in anything for you. Sherry will bring around your schedule later this evening and you are free to go to the desk with any questions." I nodded mutely and left her to continue her notes about me in her folder.

Now what was I supposed to do?

If nothing else, the bed was comfortable, and I didn't have the image of Ava's body looming over me. I was drifting to sleep when something thumped against the window and, for just a moment, I thought it was something in my dream. But another loud thump, followed by the sound of glass cracking, had me sitting up. There was a small crack in the window, so I turned on the side light to see better. The next second, something else came at the glass and it shattered. A black crow came darting for me with a loud caw. I screamed out and ducked, covering my head, only to have my hands clawed at, leaving behind a sharp pain. Glass covered the floor at my feet and the crow circled round and came diving back for my head.

Someone must have heard my scream, or the glass breaking, and came running down the hall. I could hear them trying to open the door, but something was wrong. I turned and made a run for it, yelling out for help, but the crow rammed into the side of my face, tearing away more skin. "Stop! Help! Please help me!"

"Autumn! Open the door!" I tried, but the bird hit my leg, and I stumbled back, landing on the glass. I sliced my palms and my knees as I tried to scramble back to my feet. The crow hit the lamp, sending it flying off the side table and bringing darkness. "Autumn!" More pounding at the door, but the pain brought me clarity. I needed to stop letting the fear control me.

The crow landed on my leg and pecked at the long, jagged scar from my mother's jump off a bridge. It pecked again, harder, snapping with its beak and actually tearing away the fabric of the pant leg.

"Leave me alone." My voice was surprisingly calm and demanding, like some other entity was speaking through me. The bird just stared up at me with black eyes, cocked its head, and then jammed its beak down again, this time slicing through my skin.

The door burst open, letting in light from the hallway, and the bird took off with a rush of wings. Bodies swarmed me and in a panic I tried to fight them off, only cutting myself more in my struggle. Someone hauled me off the ground, muscular arms coming around me, nearly choking off my air.

"Get me a sedative before she hurts herself more!"

"No!" I pushed against them. Mr. Hat was coming for me. The crow was a warning, but he was coming. I had to be in control to fight back. "No, please no!" I landed a swift kick into someone's shin, which probably hurt my toes more than their shin, but then something jabbed my arm and darkness clouded my sight.

Out of the fog walked the man in the hat. He cocked his head the same as the crow, and with his toothy grin, he tossed aside the black hat he usually hid his face with. Once again, I got a full view of the deeply scarred, burned skin. He brought up one gloved finger and placed it over his lips as if to shush me. I tried to scream out, but I lost control of my body. I suddenly felt like jelly, my mouth swollen and my head heavy. Everything around me became so dark that I wasn't sure if I was standing, lying down, or if I was still being dragged by someone. I had no sense of my body or my surroundings, only the demon that seemed so determined to come for my soul. I wanted to cry, scream, thrash about, but all I could do was stare at him in my lifeless limbo.

He didn't speak, only placed his palm over my heart and then pushed against my chest. Pain exploded my body as I had never known before. Every nerve ending caught fire and traveled to my center until I thought I would explode. He seemed to disappear within me, and then the fog thickened and swallowed me whole.

CHAPTER 15

"You have to do something! You can't just leave her in there like that." A voice broke through the fog of my mind. It seemed far away.

"Sir, I can't let you in there right now. She tried to kill herself. She broke a window for glass to cut herself, and barred a door!"

"I need to see her!" A violent wave of nausea coursed through me, and my body lay heavy and useless until the fog took me again.

"I'm her father. I demand to see her." Now there was a beeping sound, like my heart rate was being monitored. Shit. I was back in the hospital. My eyelids were too heavy but I could actually feel my arms, so I tried to lift them, but something was holding me down. I tried to talk, but my lips were still numb, and even the small movement I managed made my head fuzzy. Fighting against the fog this time, I struggled to move my arms. I rubbed against bruises and cuts, the small bites of pain helping to make me more alert. Finally, I gained control over my eyes, but had to blink multiple times against the blurry film over my vision, and the too-bright light above me.

"Autumn! She's waking up. We want to see her!" After a few blinks, I saw my hands and legs strapped to a bed, my hands were bandaged and I could feel deep cuts when I opened and closed my hands. A flutter of nurses moved around me, but two familiar faces floated into view.

Only when I went to talk, did I realize there was something jammed down my throat. Panicked, I struggled, but hands pushed me back. After a very uncomfortable minute, I fought against the urge to gag as a tube was dragged from my throat.

"Okay, it's okay....You two need to step out while we look her over-"

"N-" I began to argue, but my throat was raw, and it sent me into a coughing fit, which felt like fire.

"It's okay, Autumn. We'll be just outside the window until they are done." Logan reached around a nurse and grasped my arm, since my hands were unavailable. I felt like he was trying to tell me something, but all I knew was that I wanted him and my father with me. I shook my head violently, but they were led away from me, and then an unfamiliar face loomed over me.

"Autumn, your throat is going to be very raw right now, so try not to talk. We had to intubate you. You've been out for almost a week, and you kept having trouble breathing." What? She clearly saw my question, because she gave a small smile and patted my arm. "You have been having violent episodes in your sleep, so we had to strap you down to keep you from harming yourself further. Just nod. Do you remember what happened?"

I could remember the crow, the glass cutting into me, but it didn't explain why I was in the hospital - strapped to a bed no less - or why I'd apparently been in a coma. I shook my head, wanting her to explain what had happened, so I wasn't filling in the blanks.

"You broke the window in your room and you were trying to harm yourself. Your door was barred, but they broke in and they had to give you something to calm you down. You had some really deep cuts, but nothing too serious. Two of them we stitched up for you." No...that was wrong. I started shaking my head. I needed to explain what had happened. Didn't anyone see the damned bird? She just smiled and put a hand on my shoulder. "It's okay, you just rest right now. Would you like your father and boyfriend to come in? I can tell them you can't have visitors if you aren't ready." I nodded, so she patted my shoulder once more and gave me a warm smile.

Finally, my father and Logan were ushered in and left alone with me. The second the door closed, my dad dropped to his knees by my bed. "I'm so sorry. Honey, I'm so sorry. I don't know what came over me. I just wanted to get you help-" I grabbed his hand and shook my head. I knew it wasn't his fault. I knew there had been something else going on there.

"I've tried to tell him not to worry about it. And I know you didn't hurt yourself. I tried to convince the wellness center and get them to look for anything out of the ordinary, but they wouldn't do it." His warm smile swept over me, but his eyes didn't quite reach mine. "They are going to want to keep you longer now. They think you are suicidal, and something was going on while you were sleeping. You weren't yourself."

"I didn't believe you until I witnessed what was happening." Dad held my arm and stared down at my wrapped palms. I tried to speak, but my voice came out raspy, and a coughing fit took me. It was like a slow torture to cough while my throat was so dry, and each cough only made me need to cough more. Logan brought over water and saved my life. They gave me a minute to compose myself, but I looked between them, waiting to hear what they were talking about.

"You were speaking another language, and your pupils took over, making your eyes black. You were thrashing and ripping at your skin and bandages. You'd scream at the top of your lungs...I believe your demon possessed you while you were drugged." Fear settled deep within me. What did that mean? Was it all over now? Would the demon just slowly take over my body until there was nothing of me left? I'd already lost a whole week. The next time I went to sleep, I could wake up to a new year for all I knew. "It's going to be okay. I called the priest that took over for Father Daniel. He didn't seem to believe me, but I got him to agree to meet with you."

"But first we have to undo my mistake. We can't leave you in the hospital. They just wanted to keep drugging you to keep you calm, and it only made things worse. When you stopped breathing on your own-" Dad's voice cracked and he looked away. He looked worse than he had when I'd been hospitalized for my eating disorder. "I tried to get them to stop, but they wouldn't listen to me." I squeezed his hand even as my skin protested. This was too much. Tears started falling down my cheeks, but I didn't move to wipe them away. "We've been here with you the whole time. They just wouldn't let us in. We'll find a way to sneak you out of here, I promise."

It took four days, but Dad and Logan kept their word. One of them was always stationed within my room or just outside my door. They blatantly ignored visiting hours, and the nurses seemed to find it was just easier to ignore their presence. It seemed I did better when they were there. I had another fit when they forced them to leave the first time, or so they told me. Since I had been up and more myself, they had unstrapped me and gave me a little freedom to get up and stretch my legs, but when they made the guys leave I went down for a nap, and apparently tried to rip the equipment from the walls only a few minutes later.

After that incident, they didn't seem as worried about one of them being in the room with me because, if nothing else, it gave them one more person to keep an eye on me and keep me from destroying the hospital.

Today though, I felt like my old self. I had energy for

the first time in what seemed like ages, and I actually had an appetite. Logan winked at me when he came into the room and pulled out a Hershey bar from behind his back. "Thought you could use a little pick me up."

"Thank you. You have mischief in your eyes. What's your plan?"

"They want to move you back to the wellness center today. I got the priest to agree to come to the hospital to see you, and Jack got the nurses to agree to let you down in the park area with the priest so the two of you can talk. They think it will help you. I agree, but for a different reason. We are going to be down there waiting for you, and we are getting you away from here before they decide to drug you up again. It will also give you a chance to talk to the priest and see if there is something he can do to help you."

"Are you sure it's safe? Trying to help me never leads to good."

"We'll all be fine, but first we need to get you out of here. I don't want them to suspect anything, they don't exactly like me or Jack right now, so we are going to be outside waiting for you. Father Gabriel will come up to collect you so be dressed. He already knows the plan and agreed to it. Once we told him how you've been receiving treatment and only getting worse, he seemed more willing to help. I also took a video of you on my phone."

"Thank you, Logan. You…you deserve better than a crazy, possessed girlfriend."

"Are you trying to get rid of me?"

"I'm trying to butter you up so you'll take me to get ice cream when we bust out of here." I grinned. It felt odd on my face. When was the last time I truly smiled? He returned the smile and claimed my lips in a tender kiss that took my breath away.

"It's a deal. I'll see you soon." He gave the tip of my nose a kiss and then left to prepare for the next part of his plan.

I was dressed and ready when Father Gabriel showed up. I recognized him from the side of the road as he gave Father Daniel his last rites. That had to have been a horrifying night for him; they were probably friends, maybe Father Daniel had been his mentor, and he'd walked out of the church to find his body splattered on the side of the road, just because he saw a girl that looked like she needed help. He looked me over with a sharp gaze. I felt the assessment, and it didn't escape my notice when his lips turned into a grim frown.

"You must be Autumn Crowe. I remember you from the night of the accident."

"Yes, Father Daniel pushed me out of the way and saved my life that night."

"And you repay him by trying to kill yourself?" He met my eyes, and I felt the test there. He was trying to figure me out, figure out if all this was some hoax or just some way to trick him into helping me get out of the hospital.

"The night he was killed I was trying to go to the church to ask for help. I'm not sure what Logan told you, but you could be in grave danger just by being here. The demon doesn't want me to get help. He killed Father Daniel, and he killed my best friend Ava. I did not try to kill myself, I would never do that. My mother committed suicide and tried to kill me." I'd cut before, but it was never to kill myself, more as a punishment. I didn't feel he needed to know that information at that moment.

"And why would this demon want to possess you?" He circled the small room setup for two patients. I had been lucky enough to have the room to myself though...well, minus my little demon sidekick.

"Could we speak about this on our way outside? I could really use the fresh air."

"Of course." He nodded and held out the crook of his elbow to help guide me. My legs felt wobbly after such a long time of disuse. The nurses had let me walk the halls a few times, but that was about it, which wasn't much after a week of being strapped to a bed. On our way down, I spoke in soft tones explaining what I knew. By the time we reached the front door I had told him all about my mother, her deal with the demon, and how she tried to kill me when I was seven. I told him about all the odd events and the deaths that took place since I turned twenty-one. He let me speak through, only asking for the details of the demon's features.

"Do you believe me?" We stepped through the doors and fresh air and sunshine hit my skin. I expected it to rejuvenate me, make me feel better and more alive, but I felt like I was being clawed from the inside out. I hugged my middle and paused on the sidewalk, still blocking the door.

"What's the matter?"

"I just feel sick suddenly." A ragged breath pulled at my lungs and I felt him rub my back in a comforting motion. I threw up with no warning and no chance to stop it. He reacted quickly, grabbing my hair and supporting my shoulder. A thick black goo laid at my feet when I finished and we both stared at it blankly.

"Come on." Father Gabriel dragged me away from the front of the hospital, and then shoved me into the car that came to a stop next to us. Logan was driving and Dad turned around to check on me the second I was in. "I believe you, Autumn. I'll do everything I can to help you." I'd like to say that made me feel better, but my stomach roiled again so I put my head between my knees and tried to block out everything going on around me.

"You just rest, Autumn, we've got you now." I looked up to meet Logan's gaze through his rearview mirror but a bus passed us on my side, and my heart stopped when I saw pale faces, with skin drawn tight over their features, staring back at me. Every single window of the bus was full, and each figure had their mouths open in a silent scream. I gave voice to the scream, but even as I screamed, another sound came from me too: a dark laugh in the deep tone of Mr. Hat.

CHAPTER 16

By the time we got to my Dad's house I felt like my body was being ripped in half. Father Gabriel tried to hold me, but every time he touched me it felt like my skin was burning. I clawed at the spots, trying to save my skin from the burns. Dad turned, his eyes wide in panic, and held me still. "Stop, Autumn!" I looked down and realized I had long claw marks down my arms from my nails.

As soon as Logan parked, he was out the door and gathering me in his arms. I got a moment of relief when he pulled me against his chest. "What's happening to me?"

"Shh, it's okay. We'll figure it out. Father Gabriel will help us now." Dad ran ahead and opened the door to my childhood home, and as soon as Logan crossed the threshold I felt the past rush over me, nearly drowning me in the memories. All the happy times seemed to get wiped away, leaving only the nights of my mother raging on about demons, crashing bottles against counters, looking at me as if I ripped her happiness to shreds.

"No...please-"

"It's okay, Autumn, you're home. We are going to take care of you." Dad took me into his arms and carried me to my bedroom. Over the years it went through three paint jobs and still held the teal I chose during my highschool years. But I didn't see the teal; I saw the light pink that splattered the walls the same year my mother dragged me from home and ended her own life. I could almost hear Dad yelling for her to come back. Begging for her to leave me at home, to just come back inside the house. He ran after us even as she pulled out of the neighborhood, swerving in her encumbered state. I curled closer to his chest now as the memory of my fear tried to drown me.

"I have to talk to the church about Autumn and get permission to go through with an exorcism."

"You think that's what she needs?"

"From everything I have heard and seen I believe the

demon was outside before, trying to manipulate her surroundings in order to impose his will. When she was drugged at the hospital, she lost control and the demon was able to make full possession. Now it cannot control some of the outside forces, but her fight has just gotten harder. He no longer needs her permission, he's already gained access. Now he just has to overpower her and take control. The only way to get rid of him and save Autumn's life is an exorcism."

"Well then, just do it already! I have a Bible downstairs, grab it and get back up here! Do it now before I lose my daughter!"

Logan sat on the bed beside me and pulled me against him as we both listened to the argument ensuing. Father Gabriel went over church laws but I didn't care. None of it mattered. "I'll be back first thing tomorrow and we will discuss the next step-" I reached out and grabbed his arm, stopping the priest in his spot. "Autumn?"

"Don't let him win. Help me."

"I will. I'll be back tomorrow." He squeezed my hand, did the sign of the cross, and left us alone.

"This is all my fault. I did this to you..." Dad plopped down on the end of my bed, holding his head as if he was in pain.

"It wasn't you, Dad. You were being controlled. The demon was playing with you."

"You are my daughter. I love you and it was like none of that mattered. I was full of anger and it took control of me...when I saw all those pictures of your mother...I threatened Logan with a gun. I wasn't possessed, Autumn, just everything from the past - all the fear I had for your mother - multiplied for you, and I was desperate to get you help, to save you." His face filled with horror as he looked at Logan, who sat with his arm tightly wound around my shoulders. "He stood by you, he fought for you. Logan argued with the staff, forced our way into the hospital...It should have been me. I'm your father-"

"Dad, stop. I love you and I know you love me. Please don't worry about it. You believe me now, and you are with me now. And I still believe some of that anger you felt was part of the curse you were put under. You never really had control of anything when it came to Mom. She traded my soul to be with you; you've been blinded by that love..."

"Besides, I didn't believe her at first either. I nearly broke up with her. This isn't exactly a normal situation."

"Leah was telling the truth all those years. She was scared, and I just thought she was losing her mind and becoming an alcoholic." He gave a ragged sigh, and I could see his hands shaking from where I sat. I leaned forward so I could grab his hand, but he moved out of reach. "I'm going to rest. Please let me know if you need me. Logan, of course, are free to stay here."

"You will stay, won't you?" I asked after Dad left the room.

"Like anything could pull me away from you. How are you feeling?"

"Normal at the moment..."

"But?" He leaned in and his breath tickled my ear as he spoke. A shiver ran down my spine and desire filled me with sudden intensity.

"But I'm scared to death. I don't want to be. I don't want to think about this. It's too much." And with that, I pressed into him, tasting his lips with mine. He held back for a moment, but then leaned into the kiss, increasing the movement. I became lost in him, and everything else melted away. But all good things must end, and he pulled away, leaving me breathless and empty.

"What happened with school?"

"I haven't been. Pretty sure they have dropped us for the semester."

"What? Why did you stop going? You just threw away an entire semester, which was almost done!"

He shrugged in response. "I had more important things to worry about. I don't know how you would expect me to study and focus when you were in pain."

"Your parents are going to hate me..." He snorted at that and I gave him a sharp look.

"Only you would sit here waiting for an exorcism and spend your time worrying about what my parents might think of you."

"Hmm, that's why you love me, right?" I leaned into my pillows as fatigue surged through me, making my limbs heavy.

"Yup, that's why I love you," he answered without missing a beat. He placed a kiss on my temple as I drifted to sleep.

"Autumn, stay with me." Logan stood before me, holding out his hand. We were on a bridge, no, *the* bridge. I reached out to take his hand in mine, but he stayed just out of my reach. Each step I took toward him sent him another step back.

"You are cursed. You took away everything I had." My

mother stepped out of the darkness and stood before me, blocking Logan from view. "You weren't supposed to exist. If I kill you, I can be happy again." She leapt toward me. Her hands gripped my throat, and I felt her thumbs pressing in, blocking my airway. I tried to struggle against her but she had an iron grip and my vision was turning black. I reached past her, trying to reach Logan's hand but he was too far away.

I was dying.

Black spots grew larger in my vision and I waited for it to swallow me whole. She always wanted me dead, now it seemed she would win. "You aren't my daughter, you are spawned from Satan!" There was no sign of softness in her gaze, just flat hatred.

"Autumn?" Dad's voice reached me and my mother's hold softened for just a moment. "Leah, what are you doing? Let her go! She's our daughter!"

"Without her we can be together! Don't you want that? You could love me again. We were in love!"

"Leah...please."

"It's her or me." Mom's voice fell flat.

"You," he answered after only a breath of hesitation, "I choose you, always."

"No!" Logan came running towards me, but my

mother grinned, showing the sharp teeth of Mr. Hat. I got one last glance at my father. He stood to the side, making no movement to help me, then Mom lifted me from the ground and threw me over the bridge. There was the sensation of falling, and then pain filled me as I landed with a hard thump against the ground, bones breaking and twisting as the ground grabbed me with deadly force.

"Autumn! Wake up! Please, please wake up!" Logan's panicked voice reached me from far away. A haze of pain blocked him from being able to reach me. My leg was on fire, burning me slowly until I was screaming. Screaming to be put out of my misery. Screaming for all this to just end. Hands were on me, but when I forced my eyes open, I couldn't see anything. I wouldn't focus, everything was just a blur of lights and movement.

"What the hell happened?"

"We were sleeping, I don't know!"

"It's broken! Christ, it's almost as bad as when she was little!"

"We can't take her to the hospital. She'll be lost to us forever." The voices bounce back and forth through a thick fog.

"Hold her still, I'll try to push down and then we can splint it."

"Do you know what you are doing?"

"Not really but what choice do we have?" Fire, I'm burning. Somewhere inside me a darkness spreads. I can see it entering my veins and moving through me. Thick laughter taunts me and I'm yelling again.

"This is going to hurt, Autumn. Your leg is broken. We are going to set it. Okay, honey?"

"You chose her." Tears blurred my eyes, but I caught his confused look before Logan grabbed my shoulders and held me still. Then Dad is grabbing my leg, and the pain intensifies until the blackness makes its way through my veins and draws me in.

CHAPTER 17

~Logan~

Logan watched in horror as Jack pushed the bone down and Autumn's screams cut off. She went limp in his arms and her eyes rolled back in her head.

"Is she still breathing?" Jack's voice came out as a panicked whine as he held her leg still and bound it. Logan checked her pulse and felt it beating wildly under his fingertips, so he nodded quickly to her father. It was only a few months ago that she caught his eye. He noticed her the very first day of his psychology course. The attraction only grew from there. She was shy, but she didn't let it hold her back. She still stood up for herself, she still volunteered information during class, and she smiled and joked with him when he approached.

They should have had longer together. There should have been more time for him to date her, to love her. She deserved it after overcoming so much. The more he found out about her painful past, the more he wanted to spend his days loving her, catering to her. How could anyone not love her? How could her mother try to throw her away like that? To think her life could have ended at only seven years old.

Now she was limp in his arms, her bone broken mysteriously while they both slept. They were dealing with a real life demon possession and waiting for a priest to show up for an exorcism. What the hell happened to the world the last few months? How could all this have happened?

"Okay, I think I have it. It's the best I can do..." Jack looked as though he'd aged ten years over the past week. "What do you think she meant? That I chose someone?"

"Who knows? Probably something to do with her dream. She was screaming and thrashing like in the hospital. Then I tried to wake her and it was like her leg just snapped."

"It's just like when her mother took her over the bridge. It looks like the same break. Father Gabriel said the demon can't control outside anymore, but has better control over *her* now. Is this what he meant? Can the demon just break her while we stand here?"

The thought was enough to make Logan sick. "She's so pale. We have to help her. Do you have anything to help keep her from getting an infection?"

"Just some over-the-counter stuff, but at least it's something." Jack left the room for a moment and returned with a few pills and some water. Logan helped him tilt her head and Jack opened her mouth and poured the pills in. She swallowed automatically, but choked. He moved to tilt her head more, and the pills seemed to go down. The coughing stopped, but she didn't wake. Both men watched her silently, as if the pills would instantly bring about change. Suddenly she shot up to a sitting position, her eyes wide open and completely black. Jack and Logan both jumped away from her automatically.

"Nice try boys." A voice that was not her own spoke, her eyes were black as she met each of their gazes, and then she threw up into her own lap.

It took an hour to get her cleaned up and settled back into the bed. Jack left the room to call the priest and report on the sudden change that took over his daughter. It was getting worse, and quickly. In the hour the priest had been gone, there was no sign of Autumn left. She lay perfectly still in the bed, her black eyes staring blankly up at the ceiling.

"What did he say?" Logan asked the second Jack returned.

"He will report the changes, but there is still nothing he can do tonight. We just have to sit it through, apparently." Jack took up Autumn's computer chair. Logan wanted to sit next to her on the bed again, but with her black eyes staring unblinkingly, he wasn't sure he had it in him. He was afraid of her. They both were.

"Silly boys. Autumn's not here anymore. She was born for me, and now she's finally mine." She sat up once more and turned slowly to look at each of them. Her smile was wide and stretched across her face in an odd way that sent chills through each of them. Then, with a movement of unnatural precision, she scraped nails down her arms with such strength she actually tore at her own skin. Autumn didn't even blink, didn't react to the pain she put herself through.

"Stop it!" Logan leapt forward and grabbed her wrists. She cackled as he and Jack moved quickly to pin and tie her arms down like they had at the hospital. Once their work was done, they met eyes in the same question: was Autumn really gone?

No one slept that night. Anytime either of them drifted to sleep, Autumn would scream at the top of her lungs to gain their attention. By the time the sun rose the next morning, Logan and Jack were both weary and on edge. Jack had dark circles under his eyes, but Autumn seemed unaffected. They had tied her down to the bed, careful of her leg, and through the night she'd laid relatively still. She was staring blankly at the ceiling, the sight set Logan on edge.

He remembered how, after they shared a night together, she snuggled warm against him and laid her head on his chest. He remembered how she sat through dinner with his parents, even though he knew how uncomfortable eating made her, especially in front of people. The whole time she smiled, kept up the conversation, and sent him secret looks that were just for the two of them.

What happened to the woman he had fallen in love with? "Autumn?" She just giggled and shook her head. "Autumn, we are still here for you. You keep fighting, we are getting you help."

"Too late." She rasped in a voice that was not her own. Jack flinched away from the bed before standing to look out the window. This was all too much. When he turned back to his daughter, he looked like a completely different man from the one Autumn used to talk about. "Take me instead. All this happened because of me. Please, you can have my soul for my daughter's."

"Jack-" Logan started to argue, but Autumn struggled against her bindings, and sat up as much as she could. She stared straight through Jack and tilted her head.

"The pretty boy, the football star, now all alone in the world. You could have had any woman, you could have noticed Leah on your own without prompting, but you were too self-absorbed to do so. She had to go so low as to make a deal with a demon to grab your attention. She was that desperate for love and safety. Were you happy all those years?"

His mouth was a thin, straight line as he stared back at his possessed daughter. "Was it worth it? Doesn't it make you wonder if you ever even loved Leah, or if you were really enjoying your life? You had no control. I forced you to love her and even her death was not enough to break that bond. That's why you don't notice other women, why you can't move on. You could only love your own daughter because she had a part of Leah in her. Leah ruined your whole life, she gave you a daughter that she knew would be taken away...I couldn't take your soul. I'm not that cruel. Just give up Autumn, let us go, and forget."

"Never. She's my daughter and I love her. What Leah did was wrong, but my child shouldn't have to pay for her mistakes."

Instead of answering this time, Autumn dug her nails into the bed and started scraping them back. Logan jolted into action when one nail suddenly broke off from her finger. "Stop it! Leave her alone!"

"Yes, the boy in love. Failing this semester, ignoring other, far better choices...don't you wonder if Autumn made a deal with a demon too? Like mother - like daughter."

"She wouldn't do that."

Autumn gave a deep sigh. "Yes, she is quite boring that way. You really like your girls broken, don't you? Tell me, was she good in bed? You know, you've got me all tied up now. You could do anything you wanted."

Logan turned away as Autumn gyrated her body in invitation. Jack shot him a look, but they had bigger things to worry about than the fact he had slept with Autumn. Downstairs, the doorbell rang, and Logan jumped from his seat and headed down the steps to answer. Even away from the house, Father Gabriel looked like he got about as much rest as they had.

"How is she?"

"I don't know. I don't think we've been speaking to her for a while. Her eyes are black, she keeps trying to hurt herself. We had to tie her to the bed, we needed to check her leg again, but Jack and I were afraid to do anything in case the demon used the opportunity to cause more harm." Logan stepped aside and let the priest enter. "Did you get permission to do the exorcism? That's the next step right?"

"I did not. To follow the proper course for this will take far too long. She doesn't have that kind of time. Now that her demon has taken possession, her soul is literally hanging in the balance. If the demon takes full possession of her, there will be no bringing her back, and she will be damned for eternity."

"I don't understand. I mean, I'm not much of a churchgoer, but aren't we supposed to have free will? How is it that her mother can exchange her daughter's soul for her own gain?"

"Well, partly, Autumn never would have been born if it wasn't for the deal. She was born from the deal Leah made. Also, the demon messed with her life so much beforehand in order to get her to agree. Her friend was killed, she was separated from those she loved, she started to self harm and sleep walk. That was all the demon trying to drive her down enough for him to find a way in. She was weak, the hospital drugged her, and the demon found a way. Now, the longer she is possessed, the more control the demon gets, until eventually her spirit fades away. We have to keep fighting for her and showing her we aren't leaving her side."

"Of course. Nothing could pull me away from her. But what are you going to do if the church hasn't answered yet?"

"I am going to do the work of the Lord, and let the church deal with their red tape. I know what I saw. I know she isn't faking or mentally unstable. I'll not just sit aside while she fades farther."

"Thank you..." Logan watched as Father Gabriel stared up the steps, his brows pulled together.

"Is Autumn safely contained at the moment? I'd like to speak to you and her father about what is to happen next." With a quick nod, Logan ran up the steps and returned with Jack at his side. They all sat in the small living room and while Gabriel recounted what happened, Logan let his eyes wander over the room. The house was small but perfect for two people. Autumn's room was painted and covered in posters and personal effects but downstairs had one-tone white, drab curtains, and furniture that probably hadn't been replaced since Autumn was a toddler. Jack had put up a few pictures of her through the years. All that happened to her during her childhood did not seem to be reflected in the snapshots.

As a child, she'd worn her hair long, and usually braided from what he could tell, and she grinned at the camera. One of her as a teenager, however, showed the toll her life had taken on her. She was unbearably thin; if she had lifted her shirt, he would have been able to count her ribs. Though she smiled at the camera - her head tilted to the side in a cute little grin - her eyes were sunken, her hair was shorter and cut roughly, as if she had just taken out kitchen scissors one day and chopped it all off.

His chest constricted as he stared into that face. She had survived so much, fought so hard, only to end up here through no fault of her own. He noticed there weren't any pictures of her mother. Not even a joined one or a family picture, like the one of her and Jack, which sat front and center. The woman that caused so much damage was hard to hate, because she was also the woman that brought Autumn into the world. But she should have stuck around to help make sure Autumn *stayed* in this world, rather than leaving the fight up to everyone else with no real warning.

CHAPTER 18

When I rose from the darkness, I stood in a long hallway full of doors. A solid wall stood before me, a mirror hung behind me, and a portrait of my mother hung on the far wall. About ten doors stood to my left and right. Simple doors, dark oak with brass doorknobs; nothing about them gave any sign of what might stand behind. The flooring was a thin tan carpet, and I got the odd feeling I was in some sort of hotel.

My right leg had a full cast and a second glance around showed me a set of crutches leaning against the wall. I grabbed them and tucked them under my arms. It was a sick reminder of when I was a child, of the months of healing, and physical therapy that followed. My stomach dropped like

I was falling; even as I felt the solid floor under my feet, I cringed against the sensation.

Finally it passed, leaving me feeling light-headed but still solid, and I took a deep breath. There was nothing left for me to do other than try to find a way out of here. I did not know how I got here in the first place, how I woke to find my leg in a cast, or where Logan or Dad were. Did I hurt myself and sleep walk to some strange hotel? No, this had to be something else. There was a portrait of my mother hanging straight in front of me. That wasn't a coincidence.

Curious, I wobbled ahead to get a closer look. The painting was done in heavy oil, leaving behind stroke marks, but she looked alive. I felt like I could reach out and touch her skin rather than puckered paint. Her eyes were bright with laughter, her lips peeled back to show an enormous smile. Seeing her that way gave me a deep yearning, to have witnessed that version of my mother. *That* woman would have been a great parent. I could have confided in her, laughed with her, gone on shopping sprees…We could have had a whole other life, if not for this demon. If Dad had noticed her naturally, if her father hadn't been abusive, making her desperate to escape. *If.*

Time to move on. Standing around staring at a portrait

and wondering what could have been wasn't getting me any closer to being home and back to those I loved. All the doors were the same, so I simply opened the first one to my right and peeked through as it swung open. Everything in me turned to ice when I recognized the back of Mr. Hat. I wanted to run and hide until I saw a youthful version of my mother standing on the other side of him.

"Mom?" She didn't look at me; she just stared at Mr. Hat with wide, fear-filled eyes. I stepped around him with the plan to place myself between them, except when I came around, it was not the burned face of Mr. Hat that greeted me. Instead, I found the strangely familiar face of my maternal grandfather.

"Come now, Leah. Be a good girl for the camera. Uncle Tom wants to come over and play a game with you. You like Uncle Tom, right?" He took a step towards her and she skittered back. I stepped in front of her and held up a hand. "Stop right now! You can't touch her!" No one reacted to me, but a second man stepped out of the shadows, and gave a perverse smile.

"You know I'll be gentle with you Leah, I always am."

Her father chuckled. "Yeah, Markus is the one that leaves behind marks. Though I have to say his movies sell more, our viewers like it rough."

"Oh, is this becoming a competition? I guess I can be rougher, then…" Tom took three long strides and grabbed Mom by her upper arm and dragged her to him. In another quick movement he sent her crashing to her knees before him and my yell drowned out her sharp cry. I swung my crutch toward his head, but it went right through, and my stomach gave a sick turn. Was this some kind of memory? Was I just seeing her past once more with no power to stop it? The sound of his zipper being pulled down broke through the quiet of the room and I ran for the door. The second I reached the hallway, I slammed the door shut between us and sank to the ground, letting the crutches clatter beside me.

The other nine doors seemed to taunt me, daring me to open them to find what horrors lay behind. When the shock finally worked its way from my body, I struggled back to my feet and stared at the next door. I really didn't have a choice; I couldn't spend the rest of my life trapped in some hallway. Clearly I was being put through some kind of test, and I would not let it get to me. Putting my thoughts to Dad and Logan, waiting somewhere for me, I opened the next door and found myself in a small chapel.

Dark wood jutted across the ceiling, and each window

gave a painted depiction of a biblical story. There were only a few rows of pews, but it was large enough as only a few people were sitting. An older couple I recognized as my paternal grandparents sat at the front and Dad stood near the altar. There were only three other people, no one I recognized, and then a man I guessed was the pastor. The doors opened behind me, and my mother stepped out in a simple white dress that looked more like a summer dress than a wedding gown. I obviously stood in the memory of my parent's wedding.

Once again, no one noticed me, so I just slid into the back pew with my cast leg stretched out before me. My parents glowed as they reached one another, and their hands joined in a tight squeeze as if they both would never let go again. The ceremony was short and sweet, their vows traditional and spoken in soft tones through huge grins. It warmed my heart to see the two of them, both so young and full of love and hope. It hurt to know how that story would end. They would get nearly twenty years of this joy, which was a lot more than some people could say, but I knew that when it ended, it ended in an awful cascade of horror.

As they left the church I rose to follow, ready to leave the room and see what else waited for me on the other side.

Just as they were about to escape the church in newlywed joy, Mom froze, her eyes steady on the corner of the church in wide horror. Sure enough, Mr. Hat stood there, the hat pulled down over his face, his body hidden in shadow. Determined to confront him and ask what this was, I forgot about the front door and headed to him instead. It was time to bring all this to an end. When I reached him, I stopped with a jolt of realization. As I caught a glance at the bottom part of his face, and recognized it not as our demon, but as my grandfather.

I left the room and re-entered the hallway of secrets, doing my best to understand why the demon came dressed as my grandfather. Maybe he did it to taunt me, though it probably would have worked better if I had known that was what my grandfather looked like. It wasn't until the fifth door that I questioned what I knew. After dealing with two more memories of my mother - her finding out she was pregnant and beginning her spiral - I stood behind her in the kitchen as she washed dishes and put a boxed lasagna in the oven.

She paused and listened before dropping her drying rag and rushing into the living room. There sat a younger version of myself, sitting pretzel style on the floor in front of the TV. My stomach dropped as my mother froze beside me.

A video of my mother with a man played out on the screen. The young me stared at the TV with a frown that showed I didn't understand what I was seeing. Mom rushed forward and went for the DVD player, ripping the disc out and shutting off the TV, her face bright red and eyes wet with tears. "Where did you get this?" she shouted as mini-me gave a small whimper.

"It was a present. I'm sorry mama. It was wrapped and came through the mail hole in the door. I thought it was for me…" Her face wet with tears, Mom bent the DVD until it cracked, she kept going until there was no chance it would ever play again. She was shaking, and I was crying, not understanding why I was in trouble. I don't remember any of this happening, but I barely looked old enough to know how to work a DVD, so it made sense that I may have forgotten this moment over the years.

I walked over to the plain brown paper on the floor. Scrawled on the front in permanent marker was one simple phrase: "Don't forget where you came from." Mom walked over and picked up the paper, and I watched the blood drain from her face as she read it. She left the young me sitting on the floor and disappeared into the kitchen. From where I stood, I could see her pouring herself a glass of amber liquid and decided it was time to head back to the hallway.

The next door showed a younger version of myself standing at my front door. Mom and Dad were arguing. I watched as I held my raggedy teddy bear and pulled it up to my chin, rubbing at the soft fur that would one day completely wear away. Voices raised, but they had stepped into the kitchen, muffling their words. A door slammed and Mom came storming in, grabbing my hand and dragging me behind her.

"How am I supposed to get to work if you take the car?" Dad came around the corner, but it was too late. Mom already stood at the car door and was shoving me inside. I watched as Dad rubbed his jaw before heading back into the house. I didn't remember this fight, but there were too many to count to make one more significant than another. Little me looked about the same age as before, and I clearly knew to just sit quietly, even as the drive seemed to draw on.

Finally, we pulled up to a trailer that sat on its own in a clearing in the woods. The ground was littered with trash and the place looked abandoned. Mom climbed out of the car but froze in place, staring ahead at the building as though she were afraid to move farther.

"Mama, I have to go potty," mini me whispered

tentatively. She wiggled in her seat and hugged the teddy closer. Mom leaned into the open door and told her to get out and go into the woods. She pointed in the direction, but then turned her focus back to the trailer. Little Autumn scampered off and Mom started forward. I followed my mother as my younger self was swallowed by trees, and was surprised when I recognized my grandfather passed out on the sofa, a few bottles of beer sitting on the table beside him. Mom looked him over, being as quiet as she could, but when she accidentally knocked over a bottle and it fell to the floor, he didn't even budge.

She turned on his stove and grabbed lighter fluid from under the kitchen sink. Before I knew it, she started a fire from the stove to the sofa, surrounding him in flame. Then we were both running from the building. When we stepped outside, I saw that mini-me had returned and watched Mom as she came running out of the building.

"Go back to the car!" But it was too late. Deep, guttural screams started from behind the door. Flames licked at every inch of the building as it spread quickly with the help of lighter fluid and alcohol. I watched in horror, wondering how the hell I forgot about this. Little me was crying, but Mom just stood and watched the flames grow stronger and listened as the screams continued from inside. Then her father banged on the door, his face melting away from the heat. It startled something deep inside me to see him. The door gave way, and he stumbled to the ground at Mom's feet. She pushed the young me behind her. When he didn't move, she kicked him to his back. My heart stopped completely as I realized his face was now that of of Mr. Hat.

I was running, stumbling, trying to find my way back to the hallway, since we drove away from the door I came through. My cast made it nearly impossible for me to move at any great speed and had me falling more often than actually making a step. Then I fell into a hole, and my stomach dropped as I floated in mid-air. I landed with a crash back in the hallway and found I was weeping. What did all this mean? Unable to look through any more doors, I hobbled to the mirror, ready to break it and tear apart the wall if I had to.

When I stood before the reflective glass, my face caught me off guard. Everything about the woman staring back at me was perfect, much like the painting of Mom. But then my image slowly became distorted, twisted at odd angles, and the skin seemed to ripple. Then I was no longer me, but I was staring into the face of my demon, staring at my grandfather's burned away face.

CHAPTER 19

~Logan~

Logan listened as Father Gabriel took them through the steps of the exorcism and the rules they would have to follow. He was going against the church to do this, and he was not actually trained in performing exorcisms, but explained it could take months for the church to approve it and to send a qualified person. He seemed to know what he was talking about, the steps that needed to be taken, and Jack seemed comfortable giving him the reins. Or at least desperate to help his daughter. Logan just wanted Autumn back. Watching her now, staring blankly at all of them, made him want to flee.

She seemed like she was in a trance as she stared into the distance with no sign of response to what was happening around her. Gabriel pulled out his Bible from an inside pocket and asked Jack to pull out some candles from his pack. They set up according to what Gabriel told them, and then the priest flipped open the book and took a deep sigh. He opened his mouth to read when Autumn finally reacted, straining against her bindings in a desperate move to escape. Father Gabriel started to read, but Autumn screamed in a high pitch that actually hurt his ears.

"Autumn! Stop!" Gabriel held out a hand toward Logan as Logan moved to her bedside. He just wanted her suffering to stop. Father Gabriel pulled him back and continued to read, raising his voice to go above her screams. He stepped forward with a bottle of holy water, but the bindings gave way. Everything happened in quick succession. Autumn broke free and grabbed the candle from her nightstand. With an unearthly growl, she pushed it into Gabriel's face before anyone could react. The Father screamed, dropped his book, and stumbled back. Logan jumped forward at the same time as Jack, and they tried to restrain her arms once more. She punched out at them, her eyes wild as they darted around the room.

"Autumn! It's Logan! Stop!" He went in again and grabbed her arms to pin her still. She froze and looked directly at him, a small, crazy smile on her lips.

"Yes, Logan. She could have loved you...in a different life. But now, you all must die. You are all dirty, just like Leah. She had blood on her hands, and so do all of you."

"Autumn, honey, what are you talking about?" Jack moved forward slowly, keeping an eye on her.

"Oh Dad....she killed her father. Remember how you found out he died in a fire? It was her. She set it. She watched with your poor little daughter standing at her side as her father slowly burned alive. Poor Autumn, to stand aside and watch as her mother killed a man. She watched a video that was taken of Leah's rape, so young and impressionable. No wonder she was so screwed up with the cutting herself." Autumn broke free from Logan's grasp and raked nails over her forearms until her skin ripped and blood welled up from the wounds. "Puking her guts out, crying out for help any way she knew how, but you just *pretended* you didn't see. You just wanted Leah back, and the only love you had for Autumn was because she had a part of Leah in her."

"That's not true..." Jack whispered, but Logan heard a

question there. They'd talked about what it meant for the demon to be real. If Leah really made a deal to get Jack to fall in love with her, then that left Jack with no idea what was real about his own feelings. He hadn't noticed another woman since he noticed Leah in his senior year. Even when she was at her worst, he only saw her. He could never leave her, even to protect their daughter. Logan knew Jack loved his daughter and always had, but while Leah was alive, it seemed there was only so much room in his heart for her. When Leah died, it was like a whole other part of him opened up for Autumn, but he'd always thought it was just the feeling of guilt and relief that his daughter was alive.

Father Gabriel stood once more, a shaking hand covering the burn on his face. With a sudden scream, Autumn lunged at him, the demon overriding her broken leg. No one reacted in time. She hit Father Gabriel full on and sent him flying back to the ground. He hit his head on the floor and his eyes rolled back in his head. Autumn picked up a boot from the floor and started hitting the priest in the head, over and over. Logan and Jack both leapt forward to pull her away, but it was like she suddenly had double their strength. Finally, Jack got a good grip on her and dragged her back while she flailed and screamed curses Logan had never heard from her before. Her voice turned guttural and seemed to rip his heart to shreds as she asked her father if he wanted to know all the things Logan had done to her.

Jack dropped her back on the bed and Logan ran forward to check on the priest. There wasn't much to check. It was clear the priest was gone. Astonished, he turned back to her. She sat there white faced, tears streaming down her cheeks, sending the splattered blood on her cheeks to roll down with her tears. She let out a painful gasp. "Help me! My leg...it hurts so bad. Dad, help me!"

"Honey!" Jack hugged her to him, but Logan caught her look one second later. He dove forward to grab her arm before she could reach the discarded boot she'd started to reach for.

"Come on, Dad...admit it. You would trade my soul in an *instant* if it meant bringing her back." She struggled against Logan's hold, and he nearly lost his grip on her.

"We have to call the police. We can't contain her...she killed the priest."

"No! We'll figure this out!"

"You could, you know. I'd bring back Leah if you just gave up your daughter." Jack froze mid-step, his face going white. Autumn grinned with a smile that wasn't hers, leaned into her father's arms, her hair sweeping forward and brushing against her cheek. She reached around him so she could whisper in his ear. "You could have your Leah back. You could feel whole again..." Then she pulled back and stabbed Jack in the neck with a small pocket knife she must have grabbed from his back pocket.

"No!" Logan darted forward, but she was already moving away from her father, leaving him to fall to the ground, the knife still buried in his neck. "Jack, don't pull it out, leave it-"

It was too late. In shock, Jack pulled the knife back and blood spurted from his neck, shooting out in pulses. All the color drained from his face. He looked down at the knife in his hand before he fell over, and the life faded from him with one more strong spray of blood. Autumn giggled. It wasn't the shy laugh he'd heard from her so many times while they flirted; it was a sound of evil coming from a throat from which it didn't belong.

"There, now they can be together. That's what they always wanted." She turned her dark eyes to Logan, and he saw no trace of the girl he fell in love with.

"So that's it, huh? You've taken over the body of the girl I love and you destroyed the people she cared for, people that wanted to help her. So, are you done now?" He was shaking in shock, trying to deal with what had just happened. If she moved to attack him next, would he be able to fight her off? Was any part of Autumn still there?

"Silly boy. Autumn never stood a chance. Her whole life had been leading up to her finally giving in to me." She took a step closer, her broken leg dragging. "When Autumn watched that video of her mother's rape, she didn't understand it, but it was always there, in the back of her mind. That image, that understanding that the world was not a pretty place. Leah was happy enough, she had her Jack, I'd held up my end of the deal. Leah had a child for me and she slipped away, crazed over what that child meant. It got *so much worse* when her father started sending the videos to her house, threatening that he would take her daughter and use her up too...I gave Leah the strength to fight back." Autumn moved around the room slowly, stepping over the bodies of the priest and her father as though they were just heaps of dirty clothes thrown on the floor. She wobbled every time she put weight on her broken leg, but never seemed bothered by it.

She met his eyes and something turned inside him, a roiling sickness that made him want to run for the bathroom to be sick. "So she set the trailer on fire...with him in it." Her mouth twisted into dark delight. "He woke up, but not in time. He stood banging on the door, begging to get out as his skin melted away from his body. The smell of burning flesh and hair filled the woods. Do you have any idea what happens to a little girl who sees things like that? Then Leah got worse in her hatred of poor little Autumn. After all, her daughter had been there and seen what she had done. She'd stay up all night crying and screaming, plagued by the images. At some point, her mind pushed it aside, made it nothing more than a nightmare; but I loved that image. The sight of her grandfather burning away slowly was magnificent, so I made some changes to my image." There was a dark laugh to follow those words. "Autumn would never have been strong enough to fight me, maybe if love and sunshine had surrounded her..." she shrugged.

"Then why are you still here?" Logan took a step closer, even as every cell in his body wanted to run. "I think Autumn is stronger than you ever expected. She's fought all her life; she's *had* to. I don't think she's done fighting yet, or you wouldn't still be here. You took her father away, and yet she's still there, fighting, isn't she?"

Her eyes seemed to glint when her gaze met his. They were dark, the pupils still dilated to the extreme. "You know,

Leah didn't just make a deal with me. Her father wasn't about to let his little money maker go..." The gaze flicked down to Jack's body. With the attention off him for a moment, Logan backed toward the door of the room, ready to make an escape if needed. He'd left his cell phone downstairs in the kitchen at the request of the priest, now it could be the decision that got him killed.

"They really had happy years, but she was always hiding something. The rape never stopped. It was always a lingering threat that if she stopped going to her father, to his friends, then they would kill Jack."

"If that's true then why didn't you step in, like you did when the threats started up? Why would you allow Leah to still go through all that?"

"It was going to be hard for Leah to get pregnant, I needed as many chances as I could get. I had to allow it so I could get my soul. It took longer than I expected, but I got what I wanted in the end. Jack loved Autumn because of the part of Leah she carried. He never noticed that she didn't hold any part of him. I don't think Leah ever knew who the father was..." Autumn's body gave a small shrug of indifference. "When the threats started up later they were directed more towards Autumn, and I couldn't have that. She was mine after all. And our dear Autumn is still wiggling around in here because she still has one thing left to lose. So, if you want to send up any prayers to the one above, do so now. But," Autumn tilted her head to the side, her smirk showing too many teeth, "I can't promise it will help. Either way, you are about to die."

CHAPTER 20

~Logan~

A chill ran down his spine. She made no move toward him, just stated matter-of-factly that she was going to kill him. The woman he had fallen hard for. The woman he had comforted, kissed, taken to bed. Some part of her was still there, and she would be there when the demon that was controlling her killed him. How the hell did he get here?

"Autumn, I know you are still in there. I love you. You are strong enough to win this. *You* still have the power. You still have your soul." He tried to talk past the blank face and black eyes that no longer belonged to Autumn, and talk to the girl he knew was still inside. "I love you, Autumn. Even after all this, I love you."

"Yes." She circled him, and he followed her movement to keep her in front of him. "Yes, try to love the broken girl."

"Autumn, you aren't broken; you are wonderful and strong. *I love you* and I'm right here, ready to spend the rest of our days together. You just have to come back to me." That seemed to give her pause as she searched his face. Her eyes lightened, for just a moment her features softened, but then she turned and ran down the steps. He stood in place, unsure if he should go running after the demon possessing the woman he loved, or lock himself in the room so she couldn't get back in. The hesitation left him as he caught sight of the two broken bodies on the ground. She could hurt others, and he might be the only one still able to bring her back.

Logan darted down the steps and paused when he reached the landing, searching for her. The front door stood ajar and he could see his phone still sitting on the counter. He went for that, and was already ringing his dad as he peeked out the door.

"Logan! How are you? We haven't heard from-"

"Dad, it's Autumn..." Maybe he should have thought through what he was going to say, but there were bodies in a house behind him and Autumn could be going anywhere right now. "I just went to her dad's and...You need to call for the police to be sent to her dad's house. There is nothing that can be done for them; they are already gone. I have to find her. I think she's in trouble. Can you tell them to look for her and call me if they find her?"

"What are you talking about?" His father's jovial tone was gone, replaced by years of being a police officer.

"I have to get off the line and find her." Logan stepped out onto the porch and looked around for a sign of her. Instead, he found that his own car was gone. "Damit; Dad, I have to go. Please, call the police, send them to her dad's house. We have to find her."

"Logan!" He didn't give him time to argue. Instead, he hung up and pocketed the phone before running back into the house to grab the keys to Jack's truck. He wasn't sure exactly where she would go, so he headed toward campus, which at least gave him familiar ground. He kept searching for any sign of his car while he tried to think of where she might go. As far as he knew, she didn't have any other family. She might go to Riley, or to his house...He turned a corner and caught sight of his car parked illegally on the side of the street near Brittany's dorm house. Logan looked around for any sight of her, but it was only his car.

He was starting towards the building when rising voices reached him from the grounds and suddenly girls poured from the doorways. He ran forward to meet them and asked the first group what was going on.

"There's a fire!" The answering girl went on about all of her stuff still being in her room, but he was already running past her. It was hard work trying to get in while everyone else rushed the doorway in order to escape. Already the stairwell was filling with smoke, and he saw that with the clash of bodies, he could not get upstairs to reach Brittany, which was his only guess of where Autumn would have gone. He didn't know any of her friends, or who was on her floor, so calling out to strangers if they had seen her didn't really get him anywhere.

He started around the building, looking up and trying to remember which window would be Brittany's. He had only been to her dorm the one time, but he had some memory of being able to see the stretch of campus from her window, which meant he needed to go around to the other corner of the building.

Shoving people out of his way, he ran to the other side, where the fire seemed to burn stronger through the windows. Autumn probably started it in Brittany's room, but where were they? His heart pounded in his chest as he tried to get a better view into the rooms above. As if she felt his presence, Autumn appeared at one window, the fire billowing behind her. She looked directly at him but didn't give any kind of sign that she actually saw him. There was no sign of Brittany behind her.

Slowly, Autumn raised her hand and pressed her palm to the window, and with a gut wrenching sickness, he realized there might not be a way for him to get to her. Unable to stand useless any longer, he ran back around to the door and pushed his way through. Most of the women were out of the dorm already at this point, so he could stay at the edge and work his way up now. When he reached the third floor, Brittany's floor, the sound of screaming and an intolerable heat hit him. The screaming seemed to come from the second door, so he ran for it and tried to yank it open, but the heat must have melted the paint enough to seal the door.

"Back away, I'll try to knock the door down!" He heard someone yell back and scramble away; she must have tripped over something on her floor. He tried once more to budge the door, but when it didn't give way, he started kicking at it near the handle. Even being weak plywood, he couldn't kick it down, so he backed up a little and ran full speed toward it, ramming his shoulder and side into it. It cracked this time, so he backed up and did it once more. Finally, the door fell away. A petite blond with wide green eyes stood panicked on the other side.

"Go on!" His voice seemed to jolt her into movement as she ran forward, surprising him with a hug. Then she was darting down the steps. He was once again alone to face whatever waited for him behind Brittany's door.

"Brittany? Where are you?" He crept through the heat. With each step, he kept a wary eye on the flames that were quickly spreading, licking at the walls and devouring posters and books that lay in its wake. He wasn't sure exactly where the fire started, but when he reached Brittany's door, he found it safe from the flames for the time being. That would quickly change as the flames continued to move down the hall. "Brittany? Autumn?" He touched the handle, belatedly remembering the fireman that came to class in elementary school to talk about fire safety. The handle was hot, but then again, the entire hallway was on fire. It didn't burn him as he assumed it would've if the room behind was on fire. With a deep breath, he tried to turn the knob, but like the other door, the paint was sealing the door closed.

Sweat dripped in his eyes, and he got a lungful of

smoke. He needed to hurry. Logan slammed his side into the door, and both he and the plywood groaned in protest. He switched shoulders and rammed the door again and nearly fell through when it gave way and sent him flying into the room. There was no fire in the room, but it was quickly filling with smoke. Brittany was tied to a chair in the center of the room; her head lolled to the side. When he called her name again, she didn't respond. He didn't see Autumn anywhere, but he remembered that when he was outside, there had been fire behind her. She was probably in a room a little farther down. He tried not to think about that and started pulling at the clothing that tied Brittany down.

He choked on his next breath, but got her loose and threw her over his shoulder unceremoniously. The weight of her had him moving slowly, but when he reached the landing of the second floor, there were some RA's checking the rooms to make sure everyone got out. As soon as they saw him, they rushed forward to help. Two of them took her from him and shared her weight to get her the rest of the way down the steps. He caught his breath and watched as they turned the corner before turning to go back up the steps. No matter what, he wasn't about to sit on the sidelines while Autumn burned alive. He couldn't understand if this was some part of the demon's plan. After fighting so hard to control Autumn, why would it then want her dead?

"Wait! What are you doing? You need to get out!" One woman called up to him as she started down the steps.

"I think there is still someone up there, but I couldn't check while I was holding Brittany." He was already starting up the steps, but the woman ran after him.

"Where were they?" She didn't tell him he needed to get out; it seemed she wasn't about to leave anyone behind. They reached the top of the steps and she faltered, staring wide-eyed at the flames. They had spread and reached past Brittany's door now. In fact, they were almost to the stairwell.

"Hello? Is anyone up here?" She called, standing on tiptoes to get a better view. His heart fell with loss. When he saw Autumn last, there was already fire near her. There was no way the fire hadn't surrounded her already. The woman coughed beside him, and he grabbed her elbow. "Come on. If there is someone up here, it's too late for them. I thought I heard them on the other end of the hall."

"Wait! We can't just leave them!"

"We would die searching! Come on." He tugged on her arm and started dragging her back down the steps. He was leaving her, after all his promises to help her, to protect her, he was walking away. For the rest of his life, he would know he was *this close* to her, but he'd turned away. He tried not to think of the way Autumn had felt in his arms. How she curled her hand under her cheek when she slept. How she had kissed him, full of life and passion, even if she was shy at first. By the time they reached the bottom, he was choking, but he wasn't sure if it was because of the smoke or out of despair.

They cleared the smoke-filled building and entered utter chaos. Sirens were blazing all around him. Firemen were pulling hoses from their trucks while the police pushed everyone back from the building. People were sobbing, screaming, making videos on their phones.

A fireman ran up to them, pushing them away from the building and leaning down to talk to them. "Is there anyone else in there?"

"We think there was another person on the third floor," the woman at his side answered before he could. His throat felt swollen shut, and it was a struggle to pull in a breath. Was it because of the fire and smoke? Or was he just trying to comprehend walking away and leaving her up there?

"I'm not positive. She was on the far end of the hallway in one of the rooms with windows facing us. I saw her..." Logan pulled himself together and counted out the windows pointing to the one he saw her in earlier. This might be his last chance to save her. He hadn't been able to get to her, but it was possible one of the firemen could.

"You need to be seen by someone. You look like you breathed in a lot of smoke."

He might have argued if not for the coughing fit the woman beside him went into. It wasn't until he reached out to lead her away that he realized his whole body was shaking. They walked across the grounds to an ambulance that seemed currently unoccupied. "You knew the person who was still in the building?" Her voice was soft with concern and he felt her fingers tighten their hold on his arm ever so slightly.

Deflated, exhausted, and more than a little strung out, he simply replied with a nod. He pulled free from her grasp and walked back toward the group of police, leaving her to gape after him.

CHAPTER 21

~Logan~

Logan sat in the hospital later that evening, driven there by his father like a child. His father was not usually much of a talker, but Logan had never witnessed such silence in his life before, either. He had refused to go to the paramedics and hid away near the firemen to hear what was going on. They never saw Autumn - alive or dead - when they went into the building. He watched as they struggled to get the fire out, but then his father showed up and dragged him to the car so he could drive him to the hospital to get checked out.

On the way there, Logan developed a hacking cough, so he couldn't complain too much about getting looked at.

After having some oxygen, they kept him overnight to make sure he was okay and there were no lasting effects; but thoughts of Autumn strapped down in the hospital room as she thrashed in her sleep kept him feeling uneasy. He hadn't told his parents about any of it. Not about her being put in the hospital, or that they believed she was possessed. Not that he'd stopped going to his classes so he could stay by her side for the last few weeks. He wasn't ready for that conversation, but he knew it was coming. The police would want to know what happened, how he had called in two murders, only to be found in a building on fire. He knew the fact that they hadn't found Autumn didn't look especially good for him, but they could follow up with the hospital and Brittany to fill in his story. Though, from what he'd heard, Brittany stated she'd been hit from behind and never saw her attacker.

Brittany was okay, but she'd breathed in a lot more smoke than he had. His father also informed him that Jack and Father Gabriel were found, and well past any point of being helped. They sent him through questioning for his side of the story before his father could convince the police to leave him for the night to rest. He'd tried to keep to the truth as much as he could, but he'd told too many lies. Logan had to in order to protect Autumn, although he didn't think it really mattered anymore. *Why hadn't they found her body?* The question plagued him over and over as he stared at the game show playing on his TV. Maybe they had, and they just hadn't told him yet.

Absently, he raked fingers through his hair and rubbed his eyebrows to push away the growing headache pressing against his skull. He pulled up her picture on his phone, his battery nearly dead. Her smile was pure and shy. Her eyes were bright as she wrinkled her nose at him. They'd had times where they were happy, and those times hadn't been long enough for him. He thought of her story, of the things she had gone through. They should have had more time together. She had so many more smiles to give, so much more life to live.

Unable to sit alone in his own mind, he stood up and went to the door. His dad was asleep, sitting up in a chair outside his door. He must have been really out because he didn't move at the sound of the door opening. Logan put a finger to his lips when a nurse looked at him and closed his door quietly before going up to her. "I'm sorry. I just wanted to check on my friend Brittany. I pulled her from the fire and I don't think I'll be able to sleep until I at least see her." He did his best lost puppy face, and the nurse pinched her lips but nodded.

"Okay, follow me. Only for a minute, though. You both need to rest." She led him down the hall and stopped him in front of a door. "I'll leave you alone for a few minutes, but then I'm coming back to get you, okay?"

"Sure, thank you. Also, was anyone else brought in?"

"A few other girls were here earlier, but we released them not long after. It's just the two of you staying overnight. You should be good to go tomorrow, but we are going to keep Brittany a little longer. Okay, you have a few minutes." She waved him in and then closed the door behind him. It didn't bode well for Autumn, but it at least told him she wasn't there.

Brittany was hooked to oxygen still, and she looked off color as she slept. She didn't have any burns, though; he had gotten to her before the fire did.

"Brittany?" He sat next to her and her eyes fluttered open weakly. They widened when she caught sight of him, but he hurried to place a hand over hers before she could panic.

"It's okay, you are in the hospital. You are okay, just breathed in some smoke."

"There was so much smoke..." She croaked.

"I know. It's okay now. I heard you didn't see who did it?"

"No, I heard my door close, and then something hit me. When I came too, my room was filled with smoke, and then I must have passed out again."

He nodded, hiding his relief. He'd already twisted his own story as much as he could to draw eyes away from Autumn. If it was possible for her to still be alive, if getting free of the demon was still possible, he didn't want her immediately thrown in prison for things the demon had done. Brittany started to cry. "Hey, it's okay. You're okay now."

She nodded weakly and was already drifting back to sleep, so he stood and left her. He quickly searched the hall for the nurse and when he saw she wasn't at the desk, he made a run for the stairwell. He wasn't sure what his plan was, but he couldn't stay there.

Autumn had to be dead. Tomorrow, as they went through what the blaze left behind, they would find what was left of her body and no one would be around anymore to mourn her. She died as a monster, a murderer, and he was the only one left who actually knew what happened.

Logan got on a bus and took it to the nearest spot near *the* bridge. After Autumn had told him what her mother had done, he looked up the article about the incident. How her mother had leapt to her death with her seven-year-old daughter in tow. He tried to imagine Autumn at that young age, afraid of her mother, who clearly had too much to drink. How she must have felt sitting there with a broken leg and her dead mother crumpled beside her.

There had been a picture of Autumn attached to the article. Her face was drawn, eyes wide, despair written so clearly over her features. It had apparently taken hours to find her. *Hours.* Sitting in the dirt near the water, with her mother's body, and in excruciating pain.

After all she'd survived, it still ended in death for her. Logan exited the bus and started the walk to the bridge. The quiet of the woods gave him a small relief as thoughts of the months ahead stretched out before him. He would spend a lot of his time answering for the decisions that were made on Autumn's behalf, and answering question after question about her. It wasn't something he was looking forward to, but he was alive. Next semester he could sign up for his classes again, get a new job...Try to start over and put all this behind him.

Hell, maybe he'd finally make his mother happy and start going to church again. The thought of his mother made him feel bad for leaving his father at the hospital, but he pushed forward. He needed to get to the bridge so he could say his own goodbye. The Autumn that had wanted to help people, that had done everything she could to move past her trauma, *that* girl deserved to be remembered. That girl deserved a proper goodbye from the guy that promised to stand by her side and love her. He'd left her in that fire and the demon had won. He'd never be able to forgive himself for it.

He followed the road around a turn and stopped dead in his tracks. The bridge came into view ahead of him, and standing on the railing, was Autumn.

How in the hell?

Logan stood frozen, unsure what he should do. He didn't have his phone on him, and if he called out her name, he might startle her into falling from the edge. Autumn's back was iron-straight, and she was staring at the water and ground below. Soot and blood covered her clothing and skin. Her hair was a tangle of knots at the back of her head, and he could not see any movement from her. His heart pounded in his chest and her name slipped from his lips in a whisper.

Slowly, she turned toward him and their eyes locked. She opened her mouth, but there was only silence.

CHAPTER 22

I woke in the woods that I was all too familiar with. A few minor burns on the back of my arms and legs throbbed in pain. A cursory look at myself showed splotches of black soot and splatters of brown blood. I didn't even want to think about who the blood belonged to. The last clear memory I had was leaving the hospital. I'd felt sick when I was leaving. Dad and Logan were in the front. Father Gabriel sat in the back with me. He'd promised to help me. He'd believed me.

"Hello, Autumn. That was quite a nap you took." Mr. Hat stood before me, a wide, toothy grin taking over his features. The image of him twisted in my mind. I saw my grandfather pounding on the door of the trailer. I saw my face in a mirror, twisting into the burnt image of my demon.

"What happened?"

"Don't you remember?"

I tried. I thought about it, and the clear image of the curve of Ava's foot jumped to mind. Then blood...there was so much blood as a boot fell from my hand, as a knife hit skin...

"Ah, there it is." Mr. Hat twisted into me once more. I looked down at the blood on my palms, the soot, the smell of smoke overwhelming the smell of the cold and the woods. "What else...what else happened?"

Dad and Logan looked at me with worry. Dad cried as he held my hand. My throat was raw as I screamed again and again to keep them from sleeping.

I struggled to remember more, but nothing came forward. Logan stepping downstairs, Father Gabriel coming. The sound of a boot hitting a skull-again-again-again, blood.

I heaved a little and looked down at my hands. Blood. So much blood. It was under my fingernails. It was in my hair.

Dad. I was reaching for him, asking for help. Then I had a knife in my hand-

"No!" I grabbed my head and pulled at my hair until the pain made me more alert. "That didn't happen! No!" Was I shaking? It felt like my whole body was shaking. Without warning, I turned and threw up into the leaves at my feet. Dad, lying there. Logan pulled me away. Dragged me away.

Dad. His blood was on my hands. Frantic, I searched for my phone, but there was no sign of it. Now that I thought of it, I couldn't remember the last time I had seen it. When had my life been normal enough to pull out my phone and send a text? I struggled to my feet and was nearly crippled as pain shot through me. The pain started at my leg, but spread to every part of my body, even the ends of my hair hurt.

I nearly blacked out, but my vision swam back and I saw the bridge standing before me. That's why I was here. After those things I had done...It was only right for me to end up here again. I wished, for just a moment, that I could see Logan once more-Logan. Oh god, had I done something to Logan? I tried to think, and flames flared up in my mind as the memory of setting the dorm building on fire returned. I stood frozen.

A sob choked me. So much...I had done so much. The bridge. I just had to get to the bridge. It would go away. The demon was still inside me, and would continue to use me. I had to destroy it. I struggled forward to the bridge and reached the edge. My leg was shooting fire to my brain and I couldn't put any weight on it, so it just dragged behind me while I used a large stick to help me forward. It took some real work to climb the railing. My whole body was shaking once more by the time I got to the top. The air was cold, which seemed fitting, as everything around me stood dormant and dead.

The memory of my mother holding me chilled me to the bone. My life seemed made up of horrible things only to lead to this moment. I should have died at seven when she tried to take me from this world.

It would be a quick fall. I'd already made this fall, but this time there wouldn't be anyone else to cushion me. This time, I would end up like my mother. It was too late for my Dad, too late for Ava and the others, but I could do this. I could be strong in this moment, and take this demon with me before it got to anyone else.

"Autumn." I froze at the sound of my name. It was like a whisper through the trees and it tugged at my heart, connecting me to everything around me. I turned slowly and found Logan gaping at me. Was this the universe helping me, or laughing at me? I had wished I could see him once more, but to see him and know all that I had done, to know that I would never have his love, was like a slow burn that coursed through my veins.

"Logan? What are you doing here?"

"I...I thought you died in the fire. I came here to say goodbye, I guess." He seemed to answer on autopilot, his eyes still frozen to mine, his feet planted firmly on the ground.

"You should leave, Logan."

"You won't do it, Autumn. You are mine." The voice of Mr. Hat was a whisper against my ear.

"No." Suddenly Logan was moving, striding toward me. "You're my Autumn again, aren't you?" He searched my face, and I felt his eyes raking over every small piece of me. I wanted to cry. I wanted to break and fall into his arms. I stayed where I was, though, looking down on him while I chewed on my lip. "Autumn, come down from there."

"No. Logan I can't. I don't remember everything, but I remember enough. I remember what I did."

"It wasn't you! It was the demon!"

"That is not an excuse! I murdered people...My hands..." I looked at them and still saw my father's blood staining them. "I could have killed you. I killed my father. With no remorse, Logan. Nothing can help me now. I can't be saved. This is where I should have died when I was seven. It's only right that I end up here again."

"Please, Autumn. Your mother ran from her problems too. You and Jack have had to carry the weight of her decision day in and day out since then."

"Yes, but I don't have anyone to grieve for me. Logan, just turn around and go. I'm glad I could see you once more, but you shouldn't be here. I don't know how long I can fight this thing inside me. I have to do it while I can!"

"You have me, damnit! Keep fighting, push back! Are you really going to make me watch you throw yourself off a bridge, like your mother? Watch you stop fighting? You would really do that to me?"

"This isn't about you, Logan. It's my time-" He moved quickly and grabbed my hand and pulled me down into his arms. He caught me tightly and kissed me hard on the lips. It had none of the passion of our previous kisses. It was a demand. A demand that I fight back. I pulled away and looked longingly toward the bridge. I didn't want to die, but I would, and I wanted to die on my own terms. I wanted to die *as me.*

"Logan, please just let me go. How can you even bear to look at me?"

He gave a small, crooked smile. For just a moment, I was the girl from before my birthday, falling head over heels for a boy in my class. For just a moment-

I felt a push inside me, a grimy, oily darkness spreading through me, taking me into a fog. "No!" I shoved away from Logan and grabbed my head.

"You are mine, Autumn. You only have one thing left to lose. Everyone will know you set the fire. You tried to kill Brittany. Everyone will know you killed your father, and Father Gabriel, and poor Ava. You have no name. Logan is the last piece. I can take him too, or you can finally give over to me."

"No, no, no-"

"Fight, Autumn!" Logan shook me, but he sounded so far away.

"He'll kill you, *I'll* kill you." A sob slipped past my lips and I pushed away. Back to the bridge, back to the end. Logan would be safe if I was dead.

"Just give in to me, my sweet." The hair on the back of my neck stood up as the voice soothed me, giving me a promise of oblivion. Swirling oil inside me spread more, making me feel sick. The woods changed, the trees becoming looming figures leering at me, reaching for me. They would hurt me as they hurt my mother. They were hungry for it. But if I finally said yes, I would be tucked away somewhere safe...

"Autumn, stop!" Logan tried to move forward, to grab me as I moved close to the drop off, but vines moved like snakes and curled around his ankles. This was my fight, and this demon would not let Logan help. I wanted him away. I didn't want him to see my destruction. *Yes* was such a simple word, a word my whole life had been leading up to. I saw the fear in his gaze as he tried to rip the vines away, trying to struggle to me. He was fighting so hard, but my head was getting so foggy, pain filled me, the blood of others covered me.

"Autumn, you aren't broken; you are wonderful and strong. I love you and I'm right here, ready to spend the rest of our days together. You just have to come back to me." Those words hit me now. I'd heard them while I was in the darkness and I'd fought back when I had. *I am strong.*

"Autumn, just say yes and all this will end. Your Logan can live, and you can *finally* rest."

The vines were moving up Logan now. They would

wrap around his neck and kill him if I didn't listen. But I had the power. Too much had been out of my hands, but in this, *in this*, I had the power. My mother could not sell my soul for me. Only I could truly hand it over. It might be my last act, but it was the only one I could bear.

"No! Fuck you, asshole." I pushed back against the ground, knowing the drop off was behind me. I went into freefall before hitting the ground and rolling down the steep side. It seemed to go on forever as the oil inside me thrashed and clawed, trying to rip me apart, before it was gone. I felt whole again. Clean and unbroken. Then the ground reached up and grabbed me, and all the pain blessedly faded.

Cool darkness stroked my cheek and soothed all the pain in my limbs. My head felt heavy and wet. Somewhere, I heard Logan calling my name. Logan was there; he was alive, and he'd heard me fight back. He'd heard me say no. Then a wave crashed through me and pulled me under and I found peace.

Somewhere...far away, I heard a beeping. It was familiar and reminded me of somewhere I'd been that I didn't like. It kept going along steadily, keeping me from going back to the cool darkness.

"Autumn?" The voice was familiar. It was the voice of someone I loved. Someone who loved me. It sounded worried. Then I felt someone stroking my hair. Warmth filled me, my soul glowed. Only one person had ever stroked my hair, and he was here with me, no matter what happened next. I listened to the steady beep and let the sound of my heartbeat lull me back to sleep.

Acknowledgements

Writing a novel is always hard work, but this one seemed to fly from my fingers. Thank you Krissa for all your help, but also for introducing me to NaNoWriMo. This was my first NaNo project back in 2015. I had a completely different idea mapped out, with character charts and everything else, and the night before it was supposed to start, I had a vision: A woman standing on a bridge, telling her child she had to save her soul.

I had so much fun with it and it opened up a whole new process to writing for me. If there are any fellow writers out there, I recommend checking it out at nanowrimo.org.

Thank you Krissa, Jackie, Mackenzie, and Megan for reading through the book and giving me feedback! It is always great to have people around you that believe in you, and are willing to put in time to help you with something you love, even if it's not their chosen genre. You ladies are the best!

A shout out to my family for always believing in me, giving me the time and space to write, and always giving me support. It means so much and I appreciate you!

Also, I need to give a shout out to Freddy Kruger, the man of my dreams. Thanks for being my favorite villain when I was younger!

Thank you, reader, for joining me on this wild ride and for taking the time to give this book a try. I hope you enjoyed it and would love to hear from you! Please leave a review and connect with me on my socials.

ABOUT THE AUTHOR

Amanda Leigh works as a preschool teacher by day, but in her free time, she is a book-hoarding dragon, with a frozen coffee in one hand, and a pen in the other. In school, it was believed she was an avid note-taker, but she was really writing stories in her composition notebooks and avoiding math like the plague. When she's not killing off characters, she's helping them find love. She lives in Delaware with her loving husband, two boys, and houseful of pets.

Amanda also co-writes a fantasy series under the pen name Dorian Moore.

www.ingramcontent.com/pod-product-compliance
Lightning Source LLC
Chambersburg PA
CBHW071135260626
47162CB00003B/797